Little

Birds in Cages

All that which ye potentially possess can, however, be manifested only as a result of your own volition. Your own acts testify to this truth.
Bahá'u'lláh

Little
Birds in Cages

Victoria Jane Leith

Happy Hummingbird

Happy Hummingbird

ISBN 978-1-7395983-0-3

Cover design by Ordinary Toucan

In loving memory and dedicated to
Noah Matthews and Mrs G.

"...*that he may plunge into
the sea of light in the world of mysteries.*"
'Abdu'l-Bahá

For Dad. H.A.N.D (Have a nice day!)

Thank you for being quite simply the best dad a
daughter could wish for. And thank you for reading
the first seven chapters of this book many moons
ago when you went on a train to Birmingham.
You were so very encouraging and full of praise!
I love you.

CHAPTER 1

MELANIE

Dear Diary,

Picture this. Me, with my hand in someone else's bag, stealing chocolate! I had Jane's Addiction's latest song, 'Been Caught Stealing' playing in my mind whilst I was doing it. What a great tune for such a lousy act. I feel like a total idiot. Melanie Aurelie Stoakes; fifteen years young, loner-girl, sister to one annoying brother, total loser, thief... and dad-less. Is this really all I am?

Melanie frantically chewed an already frayed purple biro lid on the pebble-dash steps outside the music block at school, trying not to wince as a fierce wind whipped greasy long, copper hair into her scowling face, her brow aching and lined with creases from frowning too much. She doodled around the words on the paper, making sure swirls cascaded from the end of each letter. She made a mental note to add the pages to her diary later and suddenly heard her mum's voice, echoing in her mind.

Your face'll stick like that if the wind blows... smile Pel Mel!

Melanie flattened the sheets of paper with her elbow as they danced and tried to jump up out of her grasp to escape and continued to write.

Well it's practically gale force today so maybe this'll be my face forever! It's my unlucky day, that's for sure.

At break-times, there was nothing else *to* do, than to sit on her own, writing notes for her diary, pausing only to glare at the girls in her class who ran around like five-year olds and huddled under a multitude of coloured umbrellas that kept turning inside out in the wind, laughing, chatting and joking with each other in the playground. She closed her eyes and allowed her mind to zone out the noise and momentarily infuse with the most beautiful music she had ever heard, music her dad had played to her, *just her,* before he left.

Dad... What are you doing right now?

She wished he could hear her thoughts. Maybe he could.

"Listen to this, Mel...", he'd said one evening as they'd sat together. "It'll fill your soul right up." He'd showed her the record cover, which read *Byzantine – A Capella:*

Female. She'd been transfixed and felt herself flying above the clouds, singing with lost angel souls trying to find their way back home.

She now imagined the girls in the playground moving in slow-motion, in time to the rise and fall of soaring monophonic vocals, their umbrellas pulsing toward her like jellyfish rising up in the ocean. The music echoed in her ears as if she was standing in a cathedral, surrounded by women who wove their hands up like flames in a fire. As quickly as it had come, the melody transformed into the whistling wind and disappeared. As did the image of her dad.

Melanie snapped back to reality and wondered how long the girls were going to keep ignoring her. She carried on writing, noticing a blister forming where she was pressing too hard on her thumb.

I couldn't help it. I was starving. So that's it now. The entire gaggle of witches from 10SW have decided to blank me. Thanks a lot, Shannon Hargrave!!! Just my luck that two Parker pens (who brings those to school? What the heck is wrong with a biro?) and a purse with some money have also mysteriously disappeared, so of course I've been framed for the lot. I can't be bothered to tell them I'm innocent because I guess it's only partly true. I really hope my mum doesn't find out. She is going to kill me.

A spiky feeling of guilt hung around her belly making her insides churn a little. *How could I be so stupid,* she thought.

Melanie reached into her bag and felt for the apple she knew was in there, somewhere amongst the books and papers. She rubbed it on her coat, as her dad once taught her, to make it look shiny then sunk her teeth into the green skin. The insides were mushy and bruised. They always were. Her mum's voice came to mind again. "It's fruit sugar! Just eat it!"

It was so cold outside that the apple felt like it had been plucked from the depths of an iceberg. The chill seared into her teeth making them ache well into her jaw. She put it back into her bag, her stomach growling, feeling like it was flipping over.

It hadn't always been this way. When Melanie had arrived at school a couple of years back, at first she'd been welcomed and the girls had practically fallen over themselves to be her friend. But the cracks soon started to appear as they always did when she started a new school. She knew this was partly her fault. She couldn't help but complain about them, seeing all their faults blazing brightly like bonfires that edged ever nearer to her. She didn't want to get burned by their idiotic ways.

"They are all utter imbeciles," she'd whined, as her mum crunched a rusty tin-opener around a can of corned beef.

"Every day there's just this... drama! Arguing over pop-stars and boys, going to parties, being part of cliques, who's wearing what and...who cares?! And you know ALL the latest diets are the main topics of conversations unless we're debating in English class of course and at least then they talk about more important things, like, I dunno! Vivisection and equal rights? Ugh! I've got no time for it!"

Angela Stoakes had raised an eye-brow during Melanie's rant and had said, with a slight disapproving tone, "Mel... can you help me with dinner? Come on! I don't want to do this all myself when there's a pair of extra hands in the room!"

Melanie had ignored her and continued. "I even hear them talking about me! It's like they don't even try to do it behind my back anymore. They said something... something about Dad. I just flipped. They said I was *mad like my dad* or something pathetic like that. How did they even know anything as I haven't said a word to anyone! Mum! Mum, are you even listening? I have tried Mum, honestly I have.... I'm better off just being on my own at break times."

Angela had carried on with dinner, listening silently

and letting her daughter have her moan. She'd served up the slices of corned beef and mounds of mashed potatoes on mismatching plates, glancing at Melanie, watching her wrinkle her nose in disgust, marvelling for just a moment that she had a fifteen year-old in the house.

"Just keep your head down in class Pel Mel, get on with what you need to do and ignore the others. Now, help me get Saul to the table will you?" Melanie had shrugged and spent the next ten minutes trying to coax her brother to the kitchen with games and a chase.

At school, slowly but surely, Melanie had moved away from the girls in her form. Sure, she had some secret fantasies, still half-believed in the tooth fairy (or wanted to) and had crushes of her own but she knew she'd never be crazy enough to share them. And she never, ever talked about her dad. She wasn't a hundred per cent sure what was going on with him herself. She knew she missed him. And that she also hated him right now for not being here when she needed him most.

The girls had always gone on at her, trying to get information about whether she'd kissed anyone or who she liked that week.

Hyenas the lot of them, jackals, making a nuisance of themselves, poking their noses into business that had nothing to do with them.

Not sharing though came at a price. Not sharing meant *not bonding*. She knew that. But she wasn't taking any chances. Telling the girls even one iota of personal information would result in it being repeated at some point, she was certain. There was always some drama going on and it was always over relationships. Being in the middle of it was a big, fat no-no.

Melanie swore to herself as the wind increased to an even greater howling pitch, hurtling and huffing its way through the playground, whipping up dust twisters, whistling mockingly at her.

"Freaky May weather!" she said to no-one.

The cement mixer was churning rhythmically in a neighbouring car-park and she found her foot tapping, her fingers itching to bang on something. Her knees would have to do. She put her hood up from her duffle coat that inspired a taunt of "Hey, Paddington!" at least once daily. Puffer jackets, not duffels, were 'in' this year. She folded her body into itself as much as possible. Her legs ached from the cold and she could feel the hairs stand up on her calves. She'd tried to shave them once but didn't know you were meant to do the whole leg so she'd used her mum's old razor, and dry shaved just the front.

"Blimey, Pel Mel! It's full of hair! I can't imagine it was Saul so it must've been you!"

She sighed and clicked her pen on her teeth that still ached before venting more of her thoughts onto paper.

UGH! I was so embarrassed when my mum found the razor.

Why did I pretend it wasn't me? I'll have to rinse it next time.

If there is a next time! I got such a skanky itchy rash after, I'm never shaving again!

Well, I never thought I would say this but I can't wait for the weekend! I hate the way they all stare at me now like I am some sort of freak. I guess I feel like that a lot of the time so I can't blame them. It was bad enough already. Look at them, showing off to the sixth form boys, hiking up their skirts and being typical girly girls. Look at you, Rachel Shill, showing your perfect legs to nobody! Sorry, not sorry. No one's watching you Rachel you absolute idiot!!!! Well apart from me. Why did we move here of all places for pity's sake? You are all so annoying! I would always make an exception for Tim Jones though. He always looks so... well, I am not sure! He just looks so nice from a distance. I can see him now, shirt sticking out from under his jumper, no coat like the rest of them. I love his hair and the way he looks. I reckon he plays in a band... guitarist maybe? He looked at me once and I swear I felt I was going to vomit.

In a good way. Who am I kidding? Ha! Am I really a girly girl underneath? What on earth does that mean anyway? Here I go again, blabbering on and on as mum would say. Melanie Pel Mel Stoakes, you are also an idiot! You don't have a chance in hell with Tim or anyone for that matter. Ugh! Literally hate my life... going home won't be much of an improvement but anything, ANYTHING is better than being at school. Really hope that my dad can feel how unhappy I am right now. I cannot believe he actually checked himself in to the hospital or whatever they call it. Maybe I won't be here anymore when he comes back... if he comes back that is. OK now I feel bad. I guess he didn't have a choice... did he?

Melanie could feel goose-bumps rising up on her arms. She shivered and wrapped her body around her legs to protect her from the increasing cold when one of the pages from her notes, filled with spidery script, slyly, unnoticed, flitted down the steps playfully and danced closer to the group of girls who were now spinning wildly, laughing breathlessly as they dizzily knocked into each other on purpose.

Occasionally, they glanced over at Melanie, tossing their curls, fringes, bobs and plaits in the afternoon tumult of leaves, dust and random spits of rain. She tried to will the music back but it was gone.

Most of the girls in her class were trying hard to act way older than their age. They would boast about the drinks they'd managed to sneak from their parents' stash on the weekend, the boys they'd managed to get to kiss them or more… she hated all of that. It reminded her too much of her own parents who must have been like this at school. She shuddered when she thought about them being young and dating.

Some of the girls were not wearing their coats as they complained that their puffer jackets made them look like the Marshmallow man from Ghostbusters. Their teeth were chattering and they were clearly freezing. Melanie sighed and had a wave of feeling sorry for herself even though she knew she'd put herself in this position. She continued to write, not noticing the lost paper which by now was dancing further towards the mob.

I am pretty sure no-one else here knows the pain of being utterly alone. No-one will ever know what it is like to walk down corridors and have people whisper behind your back.

(Unless you're Rosie Witherby from Year 9. Poor girl. Oh my God am I like Rosie Witherby????) No-one will know what it is like to have an EGG thrown at your head from the top deck of the school bus as you walk alongside it. Yes, that happened. Only once mind you but it was probably the most embarrassingly awful thing that ever happened to me.

Melanie had been furious at the time, swiping at her hair and swearing after the bus as if it had been the culprit itself. As it had rolled away, smoke puffing from its exhausts, an elderly woman, who sat on the opposite side of the road in a bus shelter covered in tag names and swear words, had watched Melanie carefully. As Melanie raged, her arms flailing, the woman had smiled and waved her cane in a friendly greeting. It looked like she was at a rock concert. Melanie didn't know who was behind the heinous crime but the person who shouted what sounded like "Ginnngg-gerrrrr!!!!!" before she felt the crack and the blow and then the egg's contents glooping over her head, certainly sounded like Rachel.

Rachel had started school the same time as Melanie. The rest of the class had already formed friendship groups but Rachel soon wove her way in whilst Melanie was side-lined. She'd tried to initiate some decent conversations about the music she liked but no-one had heard of *The King of Elfland's Daughter* and were more into Bros than Pink Floyd. Music was a big deal in her class and people were starting to hang out more due to who you did and didn't like. You'd hear people randomly saying to each other down the corridors,

"Are you into The Cure?"

"Nah… too depressing. Tiffany?"

"Are you joking me? Give me The Smiths any day."

"I like the B side of *When Will I be Famous*… have you heard it?"

"I don't have a record player… just a tape player. I want one though…"

There were new bands coming on the scene every day and it mattered.

Rachel had been the first one to get bottle caps on her shoes and whatever she did, nearly everyone followed suit.

Vomit-worthy.

It's such a cliché considered Melanie. *We represent all the personality types. The followers, the loners, the mean girls and the ones who are just plain stupid.*

Melanie thought Rachel to be one of the pretty girls although the way she acted made her features seem mean.

"Obviously pretty," she'd said to her mum.

"What does that even mean?" her mum had replied, shaking out the rug before she ran the vacuum over it.

"You know… all her features are in the right place, the right proportions of everything…"

"Haven't you heard, Pel Mel, that beauty is in the eye of

the beholder? You're beautiful darling too... now help me get the last bit of dirt out."

But Melanie couldn't help but wish for long, perfectly silky, jet-black hair like Rachel's, that swished as she walked.

Rachel always, *always* wore a pink feather clip at the front of her head, which Melanie thought was a bit of an odd place to put it. Teachers seemed to love her as she was a straight A-student and was the first person to offer to help carry their books, open doors and fetch drinks for the lazier members of staff. She once even helped her English teacher study for her theory driving test and received a gift of a bunny holding a tin of chocolates. She'd handed them round to everyone except Melanie.

On their first day, Melanie had witnessed Rachel pushing one of the younger year seven students to the ground and shouting at her about something. She'd hissed at her like a cat, laughed and then swaggered off to a group of open-mouthed girls but not before saying in a low voice,

"Don't even think of telling. You won't be believed anyway and you'll soon see what you get if you go round making up lies about me."

The girl, self-esteem bruising already, had looked up with wide, scared eyes and nodded, affirming her silence. *The Rachel Effect.*

Rachel had caught Melanie watching the pair of them and spun around to face her, feet apart as if in a duel.

"Hey! New girl. See something you want?"

Melanie had shaken her head, mumbling as quietly as she could, "You're also the new girl, weirdo!" and had quickly walked away but that first impression imprinted on her brain.

"You're obsessing over her," her mum had said. "Do you realise that?"

"Mel's got a girl crush!" Saul had mocked, his eyes glinting.

"And so what if I have? Well…let me show you what I have to put up with, OK?" Melanie had said, pushing her brother lightly and he'd laughed and rolled his head back. She'd strutted around the kitchen, grabbing a tea-towel and putting it round her shoulders.

"My name is Rachel… hark at me with my striking, *piercing* blue eyes and *perfect* skin that shimmers and sparkles like a mermaid… or maybe a siren… to be more apt. Sadly… I only show my beauty on the *outside* only. I wear my skirt a little *shorter* than everyone else, my blazer is fastened with this one little button at the top and my tie is always worn with the thinnest part showing, which technically, *technically* is an isolation offence for most people… but not me! Because I am Rachel Shill! Queen of the School!"

"Enough Pel Mel!" her mum had said trying not to laugh. "Perhaps you should have taken the drama option instead of art?"

"Well, she seems to have it all sometimes," Mel had grumbled. "She had those cool bubble socks on today that look really good with ankle boots… everyone has them except me."

"Which makes you… original! Come on, get over yourself. You can't have it both ways Pel Mel, complaining one minute then wishing you were more like them the next."

Melanie snapped back to the cold and the wind and glared at the girls, her pen beginning to bend a little as she pressed harder, pursing her lips are she wrote.

I hate to say this but I feel like such a skank next to Rachel. There's me, with my grey tights with fluff coming off them and shoes from Shoe Value which is where all shoes basically go to die and are re-sold into shoes where the heels come off as soon as you look at them. Skirt from the market. Embarrassing. Skin full of pock marks and angry spots that look like someone threw a pizza at my face. Sickening. Oh look… the Queen is starting to speak. What on earth is she holding? Hang on… DEAR DIARY! NOOOO!

Melanie suddenly spied Rachel raising her foot in the air and stamping it down on the escapee paper that was now undulating around the legs of the girls. She gasped and cursed the wind through gritted teeth as she realised what had happened.

"If you're going to be against me too, then at least don't give my notes to Rachel... anyone but Rachel! Oh my God, *oh my God!*"

"Gather round, gather round!" Rachel triumphantly called, welcoming the crowd to the circus, holding the precious piece of paper above her head and smiling a saccharine smile across to Melanie. "What have we got here then? Listen carefully as I think the classroom thief has got a lot to say about us more law-abiding citizens."

Well, we do have something in common... we both love a bit of drama thought Melanie, feeling horrified to the core at the thought of Rachel reading her diary notes. She sent an imaginary tempestuous tornado spinning across to Rachel, which sucked her up and spat her outside the school gates straight into the rubbish bin. However, not being well-versed in any form of witchcraft, she settled for a weak scowl. Inside, she felt as if her stomach was being wrung out and pinned up to dry as Rachel skimmed over the crumpled page, looking dangerously at Melanie. She quietly let her entourage read the diary extract then ripped it into pieces, scattering them on the grey tarmac as if feeding a pack of hungry, bloodthirsty hounds. Her friends, overexcited, tried to catch bits of paper with their boots, squealing like baby pigs as they stamped around joyfully.

"Oi!" a gruff voice yelled and they all looked up towards the main block to see an angry man half-hanging out of the window from the third floor. Mr Roody, the *headmaster,* as he liked to call himself, was shaking his finger whilst trying to keep a hold of the window as it was nearly forced off its hinges by the now wailing wind. *He looks pretty ridiculous* Melanie thought. *Ridiculous and bloody terrifying.*

The playground jostlers and even the lads from the sixth form quickly made way for a very red-faced Mr Roody as he trundled over yet marched straight past the wide-eyed girls and instead placed himself squarely in front of Melanie. Rachel's face flushed scarlet, thinking he'd seen her chucking paper in the playground and she nudged her friends at this sudden twist of fate.

"Don't you have some explaining to do in my office, young lady?" Mr Roody asked a little too roughly. He appeared to have a bit of gravy on his chin. Melanie suddenly remembered. *How could I be so stupid* she thought.

"I, er, I forgot Mr Roody..." The words sounded feeble and were almost inaudible to the towering giant. Incensed further by this apparent show of defiance, Mr Roody's nostrils flared and had he been a real dragon, smoke would have certainly poured out of his ears.

"Get to my office, now!" he roared but the wind seemed to carry his words and make them feel smaller, quieter.

Melanie clumsily grabbed her rucksack, which was covered in dust and dirt. It was not properly tied at the top and one of the clips was broken so the apple came tumbling out.

Ground, swallow me up now, thought Melanie.

"Leave it!" Mr Roody ordered and marched off ahead, getting side-tracked by two boys who'd just started pulling each others' jumpers. Melanie glanced over to the girls who she thought couldn't possibly get any closer to each other, as she made the longest journey of her life across the playground to the main entrance. The boys began to disperse now the fun had ended, and Melanie was surprised to hear a couple of well-meaning pupils venture a few words of, "Good luck… you're gonna need it!".

Rachel held a remaining piece of torn paper and gave Melanie what looked like a half-smile. Maybe it was a grimace.

"You're a lousy writer, Mel… and a thief," she added. Melanie's heart suddenly started thumping hard in her chest and she felt bubbles rise in her throat.

Oh no, not now!

She breathed slowly as her mum had taught her, in and out, through her nose, and counted to ten. She thought she saw another look on Rachel's face. Was it pity? Everyone knew how awful and unfair Mr Roody could be to the older kids. Rachel sharpened her eyes and Melanie sighed as she resigned herself to the fact that she would never fit in with anyone in this terrible school. Damage control options were over. She'd lost the will to even try. Instead, she tried to focus on the opening of the entrance, which had never looked so unwelcoming. Echoes of monastic voices filled her ears again as if someone was turning up the volume, harmonies weaving, ducking and diving. It made her feel like she was in a film, walking into the chasm of fire and smoke, the dragon's lair, to be consumed.

CHAPTER 2
SALLY

The nurse smoothed out the creases in her spotless, white skirt and brushed stray biscuit crumbs from the starched covering on her lap. The younger girls usually wore a pink uniform but since her promotion, she'd worn white. Breaktime was over. Not that she ever took any proper time off. She usually ate with the residents.

She peered disapprovingly over the top of old fashioned spectacles, which she'd picked up as a bargain from Misfits Antique Store in the old town. They were worn for effect as she had perfect vision. Swirls of freshly-washed rose-pink hair tumbled around her shoulders, twisted up at the front and fastened with a clip in a fashion style from the 1950s. For all her quirks, this was her favourite. Pink reminded her of the sunrise or sunset, her two favourite times of day. A smear of fuchsia lipstick covered her thin lips. She was tall but slightly hunched at the shoulders to make herself appear shorter and with one of those smiles that always seemed fixed upwards. Her nose was slightly crooked from when a rounders ball had hit her in a game at school. She thought it made her look unique.

The last half-hour or so had been spent watching 'Old George' as most of the staff called him. He had been sitting in the same place all morning. The only movements he made were his thin, fragile hands clasping together and unclasping, holding onto an object that was obscured from vision. The nurse knew exactly what he was hiding though, as it travelled everywhere with him. She sighed and opened her mouth to speak although she knew it would be no use.

"George? George! Did you want to go and sit on the bench outside, get some fresh air?" she asked almost sharply. She had limited patience with him sometimes, as when he did manage to speak to the staff he could be rather abrupt. Brenda, who was ninety-something, yet still managed to sport a shock of thick black curly hair, courtesy of monthly hair-dying sessions, wheeled her chair up beside the nurse and placed a bony but surprisingly strong hand on her arm. Blue veins pattered Brenda's hand like vivid lightning streaks and there were angry looking bruises where she had knocked herself on the arms of her chair.

"Sally?" she ruffled the nurse's arm. "Leave him be today. You know it's the anniversary of…"

Brenda's cracked tones trailed off slowly as George rose unsteadily from the flower-patterned chair, his eyes full of tears. He turned on his slippered heel and padded down the carpeted corridor. The two woman looked at each other knowingly although neither one had ever discovered exactly what had happened.

"Anniversaries are always the worst," Brenda whispered.

Sally checked her watch for the umpteenth time that day and sighed. When her shift was over, she would be meeting with David, her dad's golfing buddy. He was considerably older than she was, owned his own printing company and drove a car that was too big and too fast.

"Come on Brenda, let me take you to the lounge. Your favourite programme has started."

Sally absentmindedly pushed Brenda far too close to the television in the room, shared by all fifteen of the residents of Sunny Well Nursing Home. This was the new part of the building, which had recently been refurbished and most of the elderly people had already grown accustomed to being in there. The furniture was a jumble of mis-matched chairs and sofas. Everyone had their favourite spot and a few of the less agile residents would be lowered into their seats and stay there for most of the day, flitting between sleeping and listening to the radio. There was a strange assortment of pictures on the wall, donated by former residents and their families. There were so many that wall space was becoming scarce and it looked as if the pictures had been thrown on, all crooked, not a single one straight.

Occasionally, a school choir would come and sing or the local Granny Knitters Group would crotchet squares for blankets and make hundreds of tiny hats for premature babies, chatting away to anyone who cared to listen. The presenter's voice on the show blared over the hum of electricity and the moaning of Betty, who rocked back and forth in her wicker chair. Sally mused about David. She was quite fascinated at his family life and how it differed so much from her own. David was married, with three grown-up children. He always took the opportunity to tell Sally about his world. She always listened and nodded politely, not really having much to offer to the one-sided conversation. David mostly talked about his wife.

"*She just got another PhD!*"

"*Yes, all our three were born naturally – not a single drop of pain relief! Not even gas and air! What a trouper she is!*"

"*And she can actually climb up a rock face... with no ropes!*"

"*She's beat me at table tennis no end of times!*"

"*Her cooking is to die for... oh if you could only try her special Monday night lasagne and home-made garlic bread...!*"

Sally led the simple life when it came to food and pursuits. She ate chick-peas from the can mixed with a fresh garden salad. She never, ever ate dessert, except on her birthday, when she'd eat a whole tub of Neapolitan ice-cream with a swirl of caramel sauce from the local Co-Op. She washed her hair on Sundays and Thursdays and dyed it every six weeks so the roots wouldn't show. She listened to Radio Four, nothing else. She always slept with a little light on in the hallway. And she made her bed the same way she taught the young staff at Sunny Well to, with the corners folded in and the sheets laid exactly so. She had never in her whole life climbed a rock face, with or without ropes.

She'd also never raised her voice to anyone but when her line manager told her that she couldn't come to work with pink hair, she'd looked him dead straight in the eye and told him in no uncertain terms that she'd do what she wanted with her own hair and body. He'd looked surprised and then never brought it up again.

Life was good. And she felt a slight tingle of excitement when David picked her up as she knew she might get to hear about one of his sons, Geoff.

"Geoff? He's the kindest guy you could ever meet!"

"He bought a puppy from a rescue home and called it Honey!"

"*He's vegetarian… practically vegan now except on Sundays of course.*"

"*He's very handsome you know! Well, what else would you expect!?*"

"*Yes… his wife left him… he was really gutted. Such a nice guy!*"

The more David shared about his family, the more Sally became intrigued. Her mum had always been going on at her about dating and getting out more. Imagine having David for a father-in-law. How weird would that be? But she knew that the only time she'd ever see David, would be on those Fridays, him waiting outside in his car and her walking down the ramp whilst he watched, down the well-kept lawn, past the rows of potted plants and the tiny herb garden which was cared for by Brenda and bracing herself for an evening alone in her 'singles flat' as she called it, in the town centre. David nearly always asked if she'd met someone. It was the same routine each week.

"So… anyone new on the scene Sal?" David would say in a deep husky voice that made her imagine a roasting warm fire and buttery toast for some reason. It was usually the only question he'd ask her before launching into a speech about everything that was wonderful.

"Ha ha… no, not this week David! Same old, same old," she nearly always replied.

Her dad had meant well, when he'd arranged over a good game of golf, that Sally could be picked up each Friday from the nursing home, as it was directly on David's route. "It'll save you getting the bus once a week at least, love," he'd said kindly. She saw David more than her parents at the moment. She wondered if that made her a sad case. David always had a look in his eye when he picked her up, as if he felt a bit sorry for her.

Sally's life was mainly wrapped up in Sunny Well. There was always a lot to do in the home but some of the staff would spend longer than allowed on their breaks, slacking off and taking advantage of her kinder nature. She'd opened the broom closet once and Tracy had been in there reading a Woman's Weekly and sucking a lolly.

"I've done all the folding," Tracy had said, looking only a little bit sheepish and then she'd leaned over, grabbed the door from Sally and closed it again.

You could often see smoke rising from behind the shed in the garden and people came in late and left early. She never really fitted in with the younger women here. She was the same age as some of them but felt much older. They all had partners and some had children, dropping them off at the nursery round the corner before coming to work, popping over to see them through the gates whilst they played on tractors and little swings at lunch.

The thought of having to keep caring for someone past her job hours made her wince. Sally loved her work but was also glad when it was time to go home, even though it meant being alone. Well, not totally alone as she'd managed to smuggle in a stray cat and it had kind of stuck around. She called him Horatio and she talked to him as if he were a human companion. She kind of liked it in a way, was used to it. People could make things a little… complicated. She listened to the radio a lot and talked to herself in the kitchen if Horatio had snuck out into the garden.

"Then you take the shallots and r-o-l-l them slowly in the marinade…" announced the woman on the TV.

R-o-l-l on a week on Monday, Sally thought to herself. The work experience lot from the local high school would turn up and they were usually good for a laugh. She looked outside to where it was now windy and spitting with rain. She shivered slightly and buttoned up her knitted navy cardigan.

The only arms that would ever give her a consoling hug were her own. Maybe that was enough?

CHAPTER 3

MELANIE

Melanie chewed the quicks of her fingers nervously as she waited outside Mr Roody's office. She knew from experience that he liked to make his pupils wait. Mrs Wrenton, form teacher for 10SW, walked past, gave Melanie a withering look and opened the door to the office.

"Miss Stoakes," she announced shortly, "you may go in and take a seat now." Melanie hated the way all the teachers were so formal with them. *We're still kids you know,* she thought.

The office was full of books and papers and Mr Roody's desk groaned under a stack of folders and official-looking documents in roughly bound files, contents spilling out, glass paperweights with dead sea creatures fixed in petrified positions and a gigantic stapler that was labelled 'Property of the Office'. Mr Roody had not yet arrived so Melanie had a good chance to look around and marvelled momentarily at a collection of tiny frogs, their gigantic eyes disproportionate to their bodies. As she stood there, she could only hear silence, nothing else. Not even a clock ticking on the wall. It was weird to be in the midst of such chaos with no sound. The room seemed to move around her, a silent glacier of paper.

A pungent scent of soft polished leather combined with a faint wafting of cherry cigar smoke and strong coffee invaded Melanie's nose, which she twitched quickly to stop herself from sneezing. She hoped this would be the last time to be in this room as she couldn't bear to see another set of nostrils flaring or spit flying from Mr Roody's mouth as he shouted.

Her eye caught something she had never spotted before – a beautifully ornate photo frame turned face down. Her fingers itched to turn it over to see the picture it was hiding but there was a creaking behind the door, breaking the silence and the next thing she knew, in swept Mr Roody, sweat pouring from his brow, from walking three flights of stairs no doubt, his face even redder if that was at all possible, a coffee stain to join the gravy on his blue chequered tie, his eyebrows straggly and unkempt. Melanie's hands whipped back behind her and she had another quick pick at her nails, silently cursing as she pulled too hard on a stray bit of skin.

Mr Roody went to his desk and shuffled some papers for what appeared to be no particular reason, cleared his throat several times and stared at Melanie. There was an awkward moment as he paused, his left eye twitching, his breathing laboured. Melanie looked at him as much as she dared, melodies of one of her dad's favourite songs, Kate Bush's *This Woman's Work*, slowly weaving into her mind. Mr Roody never usually showed any compassion towards the students at this school. He always went on and on in assembly how they were here to learn academia, standards and morals and as far as he was concerned, in this day and age, almost all young people lacked any sort of discipline that had been administered freely to him as a child. Mr Roody didn't waste any time.

"Stealing," he commenced with a sharp intake of breath, a fleck of spit hurtling towards Melanie's arm as he ranted, "is illegal, it's downright stupid and I tell you what young lady, I won't stand for it. I won't stand for it in MY school. Do you hear?"

Melanie sat wide-eyed, looking directly at Mr Roody, not quite knowing how she could word her answers. If her dad had been here, he would have wanted to 'punch his lights out'. He wasn't here though. And she had a weak swing. She wanted to wipe her arm but he was staring straight at her. Everything she said would sound wrong and ill-timed. Her mouth opened to say something then closed, *a fish in water* she thought, *gasping for breath.*

The chocolate was a mistake. Of course she knew that she shouldn't have taken it but she'd left the house without breakfast, with only an apple for lunch and Shannon's bag had been temptingly open. Her mouth had watered and she'd been starving. *Maybe just one chocolate bar wouldn't be missed too greatly?* A loud squeal had let her know that she'd just made the biggest mistake of her life. Caught redhanded. Such a fuss had been created. Everyone had gathered round whilst Shannon had cut into Melanie with words like blunt knives.

"Look what this loser has done now!" she'd squawked and then released a torrent of accusations whilst Melanie could do nothing but stare at the floor. It wouldn't make a scrap of difference if she tried to explain. And it wouldn't matter now, either.

"I…I…I…" she stammered whilst Mr Roody pursed his lips into a tight line and she broke off, scowling, trying to find fresh skin on her finger to work on. She glanced at the photo frame again and imagined what the picture was. His kids? Surely he couldn't have children of his own. He certainly wasn't a natural with the students. She remembered the assembly last week when a former pupil came to give a talk about how she was getting on at college. The intention was to inspire the students and in a way they all were as they gaped in awe at her body piercings, tattoos and half-shaven head, with a twist of hair falling to one side. She wore striped black and purple tights and a crocheted black waistcoat covered with badges with slogans like *Ban the Bomb* and *I'm With the Body Shop*.

The next thing they knew, Mr Roody had cancelled double Maths and called an emergency assembly to tell everyone what he thought of 'Joanna', who had clearly 'ruined herself and her body with bits of metal and ink'. His face had turned a deep purple as he'd ranted about how they had better not take an example from her and that the Performing Arts Department had made "*a terrible error*" by inviting her back into *his* school. Melanie had thought this Joanna girl was cool but tried to keep her eyes down as the headmaster scoured his gaze across the room, almost daring someone to disagree with him.

Mr Roody continued his ranting as Melanie tried to stop thinking about past events. "You know very well Miss Stoakes what happens to people who steal in this school. In Monday morning assembly, you will find yourself apologising to all one thousand and fifty-three pupils for your appalling behaviour. Thieving will NOT be tolerated. I understand that you were caught in the act but that does not change the fact that you intended to eat the chocolate."

Despite how awful this all was, Melanie almost had to stifle a giggle at this sentence. *Thieving!* Was that even a word? It all sounded SO lame! She remembered Saul once telling their mum to *"Just chill out!"* and she wondered what the response would be if she said that now. Saul would have been impressed, that was for sure. The cane was no longer allowed to be used in schools but there had been rumours of some teachers still hitting the pupils when they thought no-one was watching. She tried her hardest not to smile as she kept remembering her brother's audacity. But there was more ranting to come.

"You are very lucky young lady that we are not going to call the police in… this time. But be rest assured Miss Stoakes that if this should happen again, the school and I shall come down on you like a tonne of bricks. And I will personally see to it that you do not get to participate in any school activities for the rest of the year." Melanie noticed Mrs Wrenton squirming uncomfortably in her chair. She looked cross with Melanie, or was it with Mr Roody?

I hope you can see how harsh he's being, thought Melanie, hoping her thoughts would reach her form teacher telepathically. *Can you see how awful and completely downright rotten and unfair he is?*

Shirley Wrenton, shorter than most of the students, tight curly hair resting just above her ears, massive golden hoop earrings that pulled her lobes down and highly polished bright red nails had only started last year. She was one of the newest teachers in the school and on her first day, she'd been addressing her class when suddenly Mrs Quickshaw, head of year, had marched in, handed her a school diary, lesson plan folder and what seemed to be a list of pupils that she should watch out for. She'd pointed to the list and Melanie had felt sure she'd then pointed directly at her.

The teachers had chatted quietly and then at the end, the whole class heard Mrs Quickshaw say, "Don't smile until Christmas! Actually, with hindsight, you're better off not even grinning until the end of the year, otherwise they'll think you're a big softy and they *will* walk all over you. If you need anything, do ask but try to use your own initiative. We're all very busy here this year, what with sorting out the dreaded work experience." Mrs Quickshaw had laughed almost a whole scale of C major and walked away still talking, not seeming to notice or care if anyone was still listening. Most of the class had dissolved into giggles and Mrs Wrenton had frowned and had tried her best to carry on with introducing herself to everyone.

A sharp rapping on the mahogany table brought Melanie back to the present situation, making her jump. Mr Roody eyed Mrs Wrenton, probably annoyed that she didn't seem to be supporting him with knowing nods and 'Yes, Mr Roody is right' at appropriate times. *You choose your staff* thought Melanie wryly who was now shifting from foot-to-foot as she was becoming increasingly uncomfortable and hunger pangs twanged at her stomach.

"Now, you only have two minutes left of lunch-break and you've certainly wasted *my* time as well as your form teacher's time. What do you have to say for yourself?" Melanie couldn't bring herself to say anything, except a very quiet, "Sorry." She knew her mum would have said,

"It's no good saying you're sorry Pel Mel… you have to feel it and mean it."

Mr Roody stared at her for what seemed to be the longest time which made her insides squirm uncomfortably. For one tiny moment, it looked like he was softening a little.

"Get out of my sight," he sighed and continued to re-organise his papers whilst Melanie tried to make a sharp exit, almost stumbling over her feet as she raced for the door. She tried as hard as she could to compose her face into a position that showed she didn't care, even tried to summon the spirit of Joanna with her piercings and tattoos but deep down, she felt let down by every single person in the school and there was not one thing she could do about it. As she left the room she suddenly had the oddest sensation of falling, as if her sight was turning to black and white, like an X-ray. Blood seemed to swish in her brain, and her head felt like it was being held under water. As soon as she reached the coolness of the main corridor, the world became darker and the hum of the school noises faded, sounding like a TV being played in another room. She fell to one knee then lay down on the hard floor and as she collapsed into unconsciousness, it almost felt… blissful, as if she was escaping to another world. She saw four Greek women, dressed in ancient white robes, singing to her, reaching out their hands then turning into stone.

CHAPTER 4

GEORGE

George sat miserably in his room, fuming at the amount of gossiping he'd heard in the home earlier on, muttering out loud as he found himself doing more these days. "Why can't people just mind their own business? I heard… what's her name… oh for goodness sake… Sally! Yes, that's right, Sally talking about me to someone the other morning, wondering if I'm all there, whether I'm eating enough, whether I've got all my marbles… none of their poky-nosed business! Why can't they just mind…"

He heard his own voice, realising with a twist to the stomach that he was repeating himself. He almost didn't recognise himself. He sounded so different to how he felt inside. When he spoke, he heard cracking wood, roots gnarling around a tree, grating concrete.

He lifted up a quill, which had been carefully treasured since his childhood days and began to write slowly in his journal – a routine he'd tried to adhere to as it freed his mind and exercised his hands. Every so often, he'd pause and dip the fine quill into the black Quink pot on the table. It was not quite the same as having the inkwell he used to have in his desk at home but this was good enough.

On the right side of the table, there sat a small, ceramic kitten, hand-painted grey, white and black. *Someone must have taken their time on it* he thought. He liked it because it appeared to be resting lazily with its paws curled over each other yet one of its ears pricked up, alert and attentive.

"Just like me," he grumbled to himself, stroking it affectionally. "Everyone thinks I don't notice but Old George hears everything, sees everything."

He wiped at his eyes, which seemed to water more than usual, with his cotton handkerchief, embroidered proudly with three of his four initials – G. A. B. George Albert Bernard, known as Georgie Porgie in his youth and now as Old George. He had been a carpenter by trade, had worked in the Navy and had survived his late wife, Ellie, by five years.

Ellie had been one of the lights in his life, with waist-length silver hair, the hugest, brownest eyes you ever witnessed and soft dimples in her rose-blushed cheeks. George was always glad that she hadn't worn her hair short, as many elderly women seemed to do. Even though it would have certainly been easier to manage, Ellie kept it long for her dear George.

"Want me to whip up a home-made ginger, mango and carrot cake for you my dear?" she'd say and would set to work, her clever fingers cracking eggs with one hand, beating them with sugar and fresh mango pulp whilst sieving flour and salt with the other. She loved the exotic, whether ingredients or places far away, although they never travelled any further than Devon.

George remembered Ellie weaving gloriously coloured fabrics, sewing buttons of every shape and size onto cushions which she would then donate to the local children's hospital ward and flitting from room-to-room, light following her, or so it seemed, wherever she placed her feet. She was very other-worldly, almost like a fairy or forest sprite.

They had both expected her *passing into the world beyond,* as they called it, but nothing had prepared him for the sense of utter loneliness, which set in soon after her death.

In her last days, George had wept at her side and wailed, "How will I manage without you? You are the star that shines in my life and guides me... how will my world keep turning without my brightest star?"

Ellie, unable to give George a verbal answer, had tried to reassure him with her eyes. She knew that he had already suffered the loss of a loved one and it was her strength and love for him that managed to pull him through on a daily basis. She secretly worried that after she was gone to her place in the heavens, dear George would let the depression take a hold of him and eat away at his soul.

Their son had missed her passing and had stood at the back of the church to pay his respects then left without so much of a word. George had never forgiven him for not being there in her last days.

He tried to switch his thoughts to the other light in his life – his granddaughter, Bethan, who he affectionately referred to as 'Bitsy' as she was such an 'itty bitty thing'. Small, a sweet little poppet, like a little doll with waves of auburn hair that bounced and curled in ringlets as if they'd been set overnight in rags and deep brown eyes which seemed to take everything in, even from the moment she was born. George had been the first person she'd smiled at, holding onto his finger tightly. He tried as hard as he could to cling on to these memories as memories were all he had now.

George and Bitsy were certainly not matched in age but in interest, they had everything in common. He hadn't expected to love her as much as he did. He wasn't usually what he called 'a baby person' but he was fascinated by her every move and would sit there, transfixed as she gurgled and cooed at him. When she'd got a bit older, they'd enjoyed frequent trips to the cinema or to the local cafe for a toasted tea cake and a hot cross bun at Easter. They even shared the same sense of humour and despite the age-gap, would often finish each others' sentences. Bitsy's dad often grumbled that the pair of them were closer than he was to his father.

"Dad! Maybe Bethan doesn't need to spend all this time with you! She'll start thinking that you're her father, not mine!"

Bethan would defiantly clasp the leathery paw of 'Gramps' and George would exclaim with equal humour,

"Now then, I'm better than her father... why, I'm her *grand* father!"

Bethan and George would dissolve into high giggles and low chuckles and then they would quickly arrange their next meeting.

I remember the moment that Bitsy gave me the ceramic kitten...

George penned his words carefully, pausing occasionally to remember the time when everything was so different.

We were picnicking at the edge of Bromley Wood and it was a glorious sunny event of a day. Bitsy shone like that sun, which transmuted the fine autumn leaves into gold and red hues, layered over the ground like a carpet fit for a king... or a princess named Bitsy... She was so good-natured and happy and bright like a warm, loving light. She asked me if calling me 'Gramps' made me feel wizened and old. I told her that when I was with my lovely granddaughter, I felt as young as a spring lamb.

Bitsy knew how much I loved animals but also that I wasn't able to care for one due to the allergies, you see. The kitten was chosen from a lovely store in the town, when she visited with her dad...

George trailed off as a sharp knock at his door interrupted his reverie. "Got a failing memory have I?" he muttered. "Well, if that's the case, then how come I remember everything? Explain that to one of your experts!"

The knocking continued. *If I ignore them, they'll soon go away,* he thought, his teeth grinding in irritation.

She was so happy to give me a present that she'd chosen herself. She had a heart of gold, my Bitsy...

He opened the drawer of his desk to reveal books and a pile of papers, entries to his journal, which were filled with his careful script, written tenderly with his beloved quill. Years on from that fateful day, George still couldn't bring himself to write about what had happened. Or was it more that he couldn't remember? He tried to recall the exact details but he just saw a grey mist that didn't allow the memories to shine through. Was there a car involved? What had he done? He scrunched up his face and tried to force the memory to come to mind but it was no use. Angry with himself and feeling weak-willed, he gathered all his papers, his past journals, all of which were neatly bound in velvet casing and threw them with as much strength as he could muster into the wire wastepaper basket.

"Bitsy!" he wept and George leant his head down as far as it would go, tears making a river on his desk.

CHAPTER 5
MELANIE

Melanie awoke to the sound of shuffling papers. *Always shuffling papers in this school* she thought.

She half-opened her eyes and smelt the unmistakable stench of vomit. She tried not to gag and started to breathe through her mouth. Without moving her head, she scanned the room to try and make sense of where she was. The medical room. This is where sick people came to lie down if no one was able to collect them from home. And this meant her mum wasn't around or choosing not to answer the phone as usual. Her mum wasn't a fan of unsolicited calls as they were often from sales people and companies wanting her money. Maybe Saul was in the middle of a tantrum.

The Sicky, as the pupils referred to it, was equipped with two metal beds, lumpy mattresses precariously balanced onto the springs along with several starched pillows and crisp billowing sheets. An interesting array of smells wafted in occasionally from the home-economics room just round the corner, which housed endless ovens, sinks and three industrial-sized fridges that kept ingredients cool for cooking all manner of dishes from 'spag bol' and ratatouille to the more simple cheese on toast and Welsh Rarebit. Mrs Wrenton peered over from where she was sitting in an overstuffed chair, looking concerned.

Melanie avoided her gaze and remembered Dylan Winters from her class once shining a torch on his face when they'd finished watching a movie during history, the room still blacked out by the blinds, and saying in what he thought was his best pirate voice, "The *Sicky* is where people go… to *die!*"

It was so random that everyone had laughed, except her. He went onto say how a young first year pupil had suffered from a horrendous illness that made her body erupt into boils, no inch of skin left. The boils had burst, one after the other, firing goo and pus everywhere, infecting everything, culminating in a slow, torturous death. And now, *The Sicky* was haunted by her ghost and if you went in there, you'd hear the moans and groans of her lamenting her lost life. If you looked closely, you could still see the stains on the walls…

A few people had actually looked scared and Melanie had said without thinking, "Stupid! It's the pipes making that sound," and then realised her mistake as the whole class had looked at her as if she was the idiot.

The pipes were now whining. Was she going to die here? She knew she didn't want to touch anything. Even the mere thought of pus made her legs quiver and buckle beneath her. Melanie allowed her eyes to open fully and saw Mrs Wrenton looking over at her, clutching a necklace and pulling at the beads nervously so that it looked like one might pop off at any moment.

"Ah, Melanie, you've come back to join us! Are you OK? You fainted! Haven't been out for long. One of the sixth form boys spotted you and you were brought straight here. We didn't call an ambulance... yet."

Melanie felt cold and sick to her stomach. She thought quickly. Had she puked? She couldn't remember. The last thing she could recall was coming out of Mr Roody's room, a black hole where her tummy should be as she thought about having to stand up in front of the whole school on Monday.

"What happened?" she asked, rubbing her eyes and looking down at herself for signs of yesterday's dinner. "Was I... was I... sick?"

"Oh no, Melanie, it smells bad in here because of that, over there." Mrs Wrenton sniffed the air and gestured towards an old green bucket with stains on and was about to say something but then thought better of it.

"Oh..." said Melanie. Her mind was reeling. She really

missed her mum and Saul. And more than anything, right now, she wanted her dad. He had the best smile. When he took his medication, life had almost been normal at home. She remembered those times when she'd sat curled up like a cat next to him, listening to his old records, the rain battering the world outside, them never needing to say much to each other to feel comfortable. He'd show her his favourite album covers from the '60s and she'd laugh at the hair-dos and massive wide-flared trousers. He'd disappear and come back with mugs of milky tea and two digestive biscuits and he wouldn't moan at her when she dunked hers and sucked the tea out. The noise of the world would disappear and the music would infuse her brain. It would always be on the tip of Melanie's tongue to ask... *what happened to you? How was it when you were younger? Why don't we see my grandparents? You can tell me, Dad.*

She never did ask though. These thoughts... they just quickly flitted into her mind every time she had a moment alone. It felt like a bunch of *stuff* that had to be sorted and filed, sticky stuff that made her brain feel like melted glue and rotting compost. Like... what was Dad doing right now as she was lying here in this vomit stench-filled room? Was he in bed? Walking around? Swimming or playing cards with some buddies? Was he smiling? Staring out of the window watching the hurricane tear through the hospital garden? What was he thinking? Did he feel in this *exact* moment, in his heart, that his daughter was hurting? Were they connected like they used to be? And if so, then why wasn't he here, picking her up to take her home?

There was a long pause and Mrs Wrenton looked keenly at Melanie as if she really wanted to reach out to her but wasn't quite sure how. Finally, she broke the silence.

"Melanie… you look very pale and er… withdrawn. Have you actually eaten anything today?"

Melanie thought about the fiasco at breakfast time. Her brother, Saul, had demanded bacon for breakfast, banging his spoon on the table and letting his head roll from side-to-side as he did when he was about to have a tantrum. Her mum had put bowls of steaming porridge with raisins on top in front of both of them. Melanie had screwed her nose up but said nothing. She hated porridge at the best of times but adding raisins made it '*the work of the devil*'. Saul had taken one taste of the bland mixture and had started howling, porridge drooling out of the side of his mouth, a couple of raisins tumbling to the floor.

The next thing Melanie knew, both bowls of porridge had been swiped onto the linoleum by her mother, who had lost her temper.

"Damn you both!" she'd shouted, quite out of character.

"Money doesn't grow on trees! We can't afford *bloody bacon*!"

She'd sounded near to hysteria so Melanie had quickly got up, grabbed an apple from the fruit bowl and ran out of the door before anything else could happen, her eyes stinging with tears. She'd felt guilty as she knew her mum would have had to deal with Saul on her own who had started crying and calling, "I wanted bacon... I wanted bacon!" but she'd got so many late cards recently because of helping out at home. She couldn't risk another one so close to work experience. Those two weeks were what she had been waiting for all year. A whole two weeks without having to go into school. Bliss. She'd wondered what had gotten into her mum. She was usually a force of calm at home.

"Er... I guess I haven't really eaten today," Melanie half-whispered. She knew she looked painfully thin. She had found life to be so stressful that eating had taken a back seat. She was ravenous now and could even imagine eating the bowl of porridge from this morning. She knew her mum meant to do well by her and Saul. She always tried to make the little money she received each week stretch as far as possible but it was never enough.

"Well, that is probably why you fainted," Mrs Wrenton said briskly but with enough kindness in her voice that

Melanie looked up and fought the urge to burst into tears. "I'm going to nip over the main office and see if there are any spare lunches left. Are you registered for free lunches?"

Absolutely not, thought Melanie. Her mum had way too much pride. She'd rather her kids went hungry than sign up for the free meals. And they were pretty good too. Wholemeal sandwiches, fruit, yoghurt and a cookie.

Her mouth watered although she still felt dizzy. Mrs Wrenton disappeared and arrived a few minutes later, red and puffing, and placed a bag in Melanie's hands.

"Now, get munching," she ordered. "And then perhaps we can have a little chat about what happened today. It's a good thing that we have some time together now." She whipped out a compact and quickly powdered her entire face then snapped it shut.

Melanie started to eat her lunch very slowly as she'd been taught by her mother, sinking her teeth into what was probably a pretty shoddy affair of a peanut butter sandwich but the flavours danced in her mouth, zinging on her taste buds, making her tongue ache. It felt so good. Melanie heard her mum's voice again, which annoyed her. Her mum was nearly always right.

"Pel Mel! Slow down lovey. It takes twenty minutes for your brain to register being full so this is a more cost effective way of eating, you know? Food is fuel..."

She looked around the room, trying to make sense of today's events. She couldn't believe she'd fainted. Right outside the head's office! Talk about causing a scene. And now Mrs Wrenton wanted to 'chat with her'. Was she going to be expelled? That would secretly please Mum, surely?

She'd get more help around the house then.

"I left school when I was fifteen to have you, Pel Mel, working hard to get dinner on the table" she often told her. "Now that your father's not around, it's hard to make ends meet. I hope to God you are not planning to go into the sixth form. I've never heard so much nonsense in my life…"

Melanie had never even dreamed of staying longer than necessary at school. She would be out of there like a shot as soon as was humanly possible. But to stay at home with Mum and Saul? And maybe Dad… one day? She didn't know if she could cope with that despite loving them all, most of the time. She day-dreamed a lot about jumping on a plane and telling the pilot to take her where the sky was blue all day and where she could drink the water from a big green coconut, sitting on a beach, the sun sizzling on the horizon as it touched the ocean, just like it did in the films she watched. Anywhere, far away from here.

"So, Melanie," Mrs Wrenton cut into her daydreams, "How was that for you? Are you feeling better?"

"Sure," replied Melanie munching on the last bites of sandwich and taking swigs of juice from a carton that had a picture of a badger and a bee both drinking the same juice. She swallowed, then added a faltered, "Thanks." She truly was grateful but her stomach was in knots at the thought of Monday's assembly. Everyone already hated her, she was sure and having to apologise in front of a load of people who are not your biggest fans plus Ranty Roody was not a great thought.

"Listen Melanie… I don't know you very well, which is a shame as you're in my form and I really should know every pupil in my class… I guess that, well, I'm relatively new here, you're still quite new and well, with both of us learning the ropes, it's hard to get to know people when you only see them for a few minutes each day whilst taking the register…" said Mrs Wrenton. Melanie eyed her. Her teacher was babbling. Was she nervous? *I bet she thinks she's over-stepping the boundaries* thought Melanie. She'd over-heard Mrs Quickshaw telling her not to get *too pally* with any of the pupils.

"They *will* walk all over you, Shirley," she'd warned. "If I were you, I'd start wearing suits with big shoulder pads and high heels. You're pretty small aren't you? If you want the kids here to fear you, then you need to give them something to fear."

Melanie had wished she'd had a friend to tell this to as the kids in her class were always sharing the best stories of what teachers had been saying behind their backs. Once, Brian Curtis had even heard the French teacher telling Mr Hicks, the sub, *to get out of their school* except using way more colourful language.

I must look a fright, thought Melanie, who was now propped up by two enormous pillows, long strands of greasy, unwashed red hair splaying over the sheet, and her skin so pale it appeared other-worldly. She had started washing her hair a lot less recently, preferring to get straight into bed at night, not even taking off her make-up. Her lips were a deep pink, chapped, sore-looking and her eyes sunken and hollow. She could feel her chest start to heave and she ran her fingers over her face to feel a fresh batch of angry spots emerging.

If anyone was to come in now, they might think I was that ghost… with severe acne, she thought.

"Melanie… I know that you had put down as your first preference to work at the library…" Mrs Wrenton broke off as Melanie looked up.

So this is it, thought Melanie. *My punishment is not expulsion. No work experience? No way!*

"Mr Roody has made the, er, suggestion, that because of your recent behaviours, you shouldn't be allowed off the school premises during Work Experience Week."

Melanie fought to stop tears escaping from her eyes but it was no use. She was done. Her face was stained with black mascara, and tears ran rivulets around her nose causing her to sniff loudly. She couldn't help it. She swiped at her cheeks with her sleeve, feeling like a five-year old.

"But…" Mrs Wrenton continued, "Mr Roody *also* mentioned that I should make the decision. I have to decide whether or not you are going to go. I have the final list here of everyone in our class and who is going where."

I bet Roody was testing her thought Melanie. *If she lets me go, well then, she'll have failed.*

"So, Melanie," her teacher continued. "I've decided to see how next week goes. We have a whole week until work experience starts and I think that if you can show that you mean business and buck up your ideas a little, then you should go. And er… it won't be at the library. You won't be able to get your first choice I'm afraid as they decided to not let students come back this year after what happened last time… I guess you might not know about that?"

Melanie looked at her, half-pleased and half-annoyed. She didn't know how to 'buck up her ideas'. She was late every morning because she helped her mum out. She had stolen, only once, because she was so hungry. And now that everyone thought she had stolen everything else that had gone missing, how could she ever get the chance to clear her name? And not go to the library? No! To be surrounded by books and writing and quiet for two weeks was all she wanted. It was as if Mrs Wrenton read her mind as she put a hand on Melanie's arm and said softly,

"I know that you did something wrong today and I am guessing that you are sorry you did it. You may even have your reasons. The thing is, I know you didn't steal the other things that went missing today. They turned up in someone's locker…"

It was as if someone had breathed extra oxygen into Melanie's lungs. "I- I just didn't expect anyone to believe me. I couldn't explain to Mr Roo…"

"I believe you," cut in Mrs Wrenton. And that was all Melanie needed to hear. She lay back, colour coming back to her cheeks. She wasn't getting expelled. She still had a chance. She'd been looking forward to this all year. She couldn't miss it.

"And what's more," Mrs Wrenton continued, "I went to speak with Mr Roody about this… this *ridiculous* business of you apologising to the whole school."

Melanie widened her eyes and Mrs Wrenton coughed a little, glancing quickly behind her as if someone might be listening in on their conversation.

"I reasoned with him that as you weren't actually

responsible for taking the other items, that perhaps you could just apologise to Shannon Hargrave, in person instead?"

"What did he say back?" Melanie almost snapped, surprised at her own sudden outburst, knowing how hard that must have been for her teacher, knowing how much her own heart pounded in her chest when she had to face Mr Roody. Mrs Wrenton raised an eyebrow and said nothing.

"Er… thanks, really," Melanie mumbled with as much gratitude as she could muster. *But this is too good to be true,* she thought. *I am like a cat with nine lives! Perhaps Mrs Wrenton wasn't so bad after all. Perhaps life wasn't so bad after all?*

"But… will you tell my mum? Honestly… please don't Miss. She'll… she has so much on right now…"

Mrs Wrenton acted as if Melanie hadn't said anything but touched her finger to her nose and said brightly, "So! It's only an hour left until home-time," and she slapped her own legs as she got up, suddenly looking happier. "I've put you down to work at Sunny Well Nursing Home – and I think you might just enjoy it. I need to go and teach my final class so I will leave you here to rest. Have you got used to the smell yet?"

Melanie smiled and then realised what her teacher was saying. What? Nursing home?! Looking after old people?

All she could think about was her dad and him being in a home or an institution or whatever it was. She would hate it! As Mrs Wrenton swept out of the room, Melanie noticed that she had left her work experience papers behind on the chair.

"Miss!" she called out but it was too late. *I'll just have a quick look,* thought Melanie and shifted herself off the bed, her head pounding. There were two people under the heading *Sunny Well Nursing Home.* Melanie Stoakes… and Rachel Shill.

CHAPTER 6
SALLY

Sally had gathered all the staff together to brief them on the pupils who were coming to Sunny Well for work experience. She cleared her throat several times before speaking.

"We only have two students from Chiltern High this year ..." she broke off and checked the paperwork, dropping a couple of sheets on the floor. Sally wasn't keen on taking meetings like this. She was at her most comfortable when just working with the older folk. She loved the elderly. She did not love organising work experience although it was rather fun when the students arrived.

She tried to sound official and cleared her throat loudly again to get everyone's attention. "Right, so we have a Melanie Stokes and a Rachel Shill – two, which is the minimum we requested... shame there are not any boys coming," she added, picking up the papers and bringing them together neatly in a pile again.

"That's always the way," quipped one of the long-standing members of staff, Patricia Oaken. "Since I started here, way back in the '70s, it's always been the girls who come and help out here."

Sally nodded knowingly. She wanted to let Patricia feel valued as she had been here so long but had never once been considered for a promotion. Then she'd breezed in to Sunny Well and in three months time she'd been appointed as head carer. Her thoughts wandered to home-time. It was 'David picks up Sally' day. He had talked about his son, Geoff, last week and how he was single, had been engaged (second time round) but broke it off and was now moping around the house and 'making a nuisance of himself'.

There was a knock on the door and one of the newer staff shyly put her head around.

"Er, Sally…" she half-stammered, "I think someone had better come and check on Old George." She disappeared before Sally even had time to ask her what the problem was. He wasn't the violent type, moody yes, but not like Ethel Gershwin who frequently threw her clothes on the floor and turned over tables, bedpans and chairs, swearing profusely. Sally sighed, as she knew she'd have to draw the meeting to an end, not that she had much to discuss with everyone and not that anyone had offered any helpful suggestions. She felt like she worked on her own half the time.

"OK," she said with forced enthusiasm. "I think that's it for now. So we'll be having the two girls in and they will be here for two weeks, if they last that long. Be nice to them, answer their questions etc, etc. Oh and can you think about uniforms? It would be good to have them in our Sunny Well staff attire so they can feel like they are really getting an experience. I'll go and see to George now. In the meantime, Patricia, can you sort out the roster for this evening's staff? Thanks."

People were already chatting to one another, even before Sally had finished. "I might as well be talking to myself!" she grumbled out loud. "They can see me but it's as if they can't hear me. Oh well, at least the jobs get done."

She walked down the hall, her heels padding on the threadbare stained, beige carpet with its fraying edges. "No funding!" she had been told, time and time again. It seemed unfair to her that these people, who had worked hard all their lives were now confined to this place, which should have been luxurious for their last years. There was the new part of the building but the rest of it was a complete shambles. When she reached George's room, she pressed her ear to the door. No sound. Was that a good sign? She went to open the handle but the door wouldn't budge. She wondered how on earth he had managed to lock the door. She was the only one who had keys to any of the rooms when it was her shift. There was a master key but surely he hadn't taken that from the staff-room drawer? She knocked sharply and called out his name, trying not to sound too impatient. "George! George? It's Sally here. Can you let me in? You know you're not supposed to lock yourself in."

Silence and then a soft shuffling sound of slippers on carpet.

She heard a massive trumpeting sound, which she could only assume was George blowing his nose using the hanky that he always had poking out of his breast pocket in his tweed jacket. He always looked well-dressed, as if he was prepared to go out somewhere important. Not that anyone really came to visit him anymore. Sally knew that his wife had passed away and that he'd had a granddaughter. Bethan, Bethany? Something had happened to her too but she had never been sure as to what. And his son never bothered to make the effort. Or had he tried and had George been impossible last time he was here? She should really pay more attention to such things but some of these folk were so guarded about their personal lives. All she needed to know was information about their diet and what pills they were required to take each day but she always felt she should know more. The door rattled and then opened. It banged on a chair which was usually under his desk.

George walked away from the door, his head hanging, his shoulders slumped, looking sheepish. "Come in, why don't you?" he muttered to Sally who frowned but quickly tried to smile again so as not to panic him.

"Now George," said Sally with a brightness that she was sure George could see through. "Why don't you tell me all about it?" She heard the way she was speaking and felt like she was patronising him. But how else could she speak to him? He often acted like a sulky young lad, frowning, snapping at people and ignoring those who he had no time for. He seemed to have a little more time for her but Sally always felt like she wanted to treat him like a respected gentleman, the one she knew was inside him somewhere. She was only in her late-twenties; how must it sound to poor Old George when she spoke down to him? *Maybe we mustn't feel so sorry for him all the time* mused Sally. *And also perhaps stop calling him Old George behind his back!*

"You're a dear Sally," George said huskily, his eyes red and swollen and his mouth and cheeks all puffy. "Would you mind getting me a cup of tea? You know how I like it, two sugars and plenty of milk. That was exactly how… how my Bitsy had her tea when she came to visit. I'd say to her,

'Don't tell your mum I'm letting you have all this sugar' and I'd laugh as her little hand would stir her tea several times, clockwise, licking her lips and looking up at me with those big eyes of hers. She could get anything with those eyes I tell you...well from me anyway. Her mother didn't like her to have too much sugar... said it would change her behaviour or something ridiculous like that."

George's face turned into a deep frown as if he was thoroughly displeased. "And... and I didn't tell her that she couldn't have two sugars in her tea either, like that mother of hers did." His voice was trembling and he smiled briefly but then he seemed to remember something else and he pursed his lips. "Maybe I'll just have a coffee... on second thoughts... no milk, no sugar."

"George – I need to know that you are not going to bar yourself in your room. Millie just came to say that she thought you'd locked yourself in. You gave me a right scare!"

"I'm sorry..." George faltered, "It's just that... I can't seem to get any privacy here anymore. I feel... I feel trapped."

Sally sighed. Her job had so many rewarding moments but she found it so testing when the residents poured out their hearts to her. Come to think of it, George hadn't said this much in a long time. He'd been so quiet lately. *I wonder what's going on with him* she thought. *'Bitsy' he'd said... so was that Bethan?*

"Look, let me get you that coffee, OK? And you know what? Later on, we can all go for our group walk?"

Even to her ears this sounded like a threat rather than a treat. What if George just needed to spend some time by himself? His own son may never visit but he certainly paid his fees on time. She spied the screwed up paper in the bin. "Do you want me to get rid of that rubbish for you?"

"Oh…" said George, glancing over, as if he had already forgotten it was there. "No, it's alright… just the coffee." He turned his face away and started to talk in a low voice about something.

Feeling worried, Sally left the room. It wasn't as if the staff just strolled in without warning. She put her ear to the door and heard the sound of paper being smoothed out and flattened. She shook her head and walked off to get the coffee. No sugar? Something was up with George that was for sure.

She remembered her last conversation with Doctor Chan who'd prescribed George a concoction of pills and a list of suggestions for him to try to keep connecting the wiring in his brain, that Sally knew George would instantly turn his nose up at. He would call them 'new-fangled' for sure. Doctor Chan had addressed Sally privately, looking at her kindly.

"It won't be too much longer, I feel, quite possibly

sooner rather than later, that he really will have blanked out much of his past. He's already confusing memories and showing all the signs... I've seen it hundreds of times before. Yes, everyone is different but the ones who have *no one* come to visit... it really does make a difference."

"So that's it?" Sally had said. "He's basically going to become an empty hollow shell. He needs more input from family and more stimulation but the budget cuts mean that most days, he's just alone in his room! Soon, we're going to have to transfer him to the institution in the old town. Sorry… I know it's not your fault Doctor Chan, it's just I can't bear to think of George, in a room half the size with a carpet that's fraying more than this one and no visitors. Well, that much won't have changed at least. I've seen what'll happen. He'll be fed by hand for each meal and the only real interaction with human beings will be the care staff giving him his daily course of tablets and meals. There's not even a garden at that place, just some concrete slabs and pots of wilting plants!"

Doctor Chan had nodded, sympathetically. Sally turned on the filter machine to make the coffee, tears rolling down her cheeks. Time was running out for George and he didn't even know it.

CHAPTER 7

MELANIE

Dear Diary,

My room! The only place I can get an inch of privacy around here! I've been listening to Wings repeatedly at the moment. Today is definitely a 'missing my dad' day. I've got Wings on one side of the tape and Steel-eye Span on the other. Mum calls it 'hippy folk tripe' but me and Dad love it. Dad always talked about how he'd hang out with the band back in his day. Of course NO ONE at school has even heard of this band or half the bands I like. Jane's Addiction have a new song out!!! I'm going to have to wait ages to buy their album so I might as well borrow a tape from the library.

Melanie swirled around her writing with her purple pen. It felt so good, almost calming, sweeping up, around, spiralling and finishing with a little flower in each flourish.

Her room was so small that it just about managed to fit in a bed, which had once been a full-sized single but her dad had sawn off the end to make it fit between the walls. A small wardrobe and minuscule desk had also been squeezed in, which her mum claimed were 'prize finds!' from the skip at the bottom of the estate that was always filled with cast-offs and junk. Occasionally, there was something worth salvaging. Mrs Stoakes had scrubbed and sanded them down, painting them a deep purple, using free testers from B & Q. She didn't like to buy anything new if she could help it. "And that's why you need to get a job as soon as possible Pel Mel," she related time and again to Melanie, "...so you can learn the value of having money... and not having money."

As soon as Melanie had turned eleven, she'd been allowed to deliver papers on the estate before school. There were a couple of other kids doing the same but no-one from her class. She'd enjoyed it though, as she had to first collect the papers from Kam at the bottom shop, who was not much older than she was, put them into the right order, then make sure they were folded a particular way before pushing them through the letterboxes. It made her feel important somehow. Kam always had a few penny sweets for her and a kind smile.

"Remember to order them from your last house to first so you can save time when delivering," he'd say and her heart would jump a little when he spoke.

She had felt purposeful going into the shop, a taste of the adult world, feeling like she was doing something good for her family and mixing with people older than herself. But she always hated going to 78 Marshwood Close as they had a massive dog that would come lumbering towards the door as soon as it heard her footsteps on the path, barking, foaming spit flying from its mouth and pawing so much at the paper she wondered if the owners ever actually got to read the news in that house.

She hadn't been so keen going into the flats either near her home as they smelt of boiled cabbage and five-day old tinned custard and the door banged no matter how hard you tried to close it quietly. The narrow dingy corridors were carpeted in deep brown tile squares and there was little light coming through the rectangular window, metal squares lined within the glass.

Melanie had read the headlines of the papers with some amusement and wondered why people wanted to read such ridiculous and terrible news.

Man Kidnaps Husband and Wife Forcing them to Eat their Own Toes.

Cat-sitter Steals 100 Cats in Northern Town: Claims she was from Mars.

Proud Elvis Fans Name Newborn, The King! Turn to pg. 2 for full story.

Did people get paid for this junk?

She'd stuck it out for a while then one morning, she'd noticed an older man hanging around in the flats, always when she walked in, as if he was waiting for her to arrive. She'd assumed he lived there, maybe had come out of his flat for a cigarette or waiting for his post. After a few days of him just watching her deliver the papers, he'd finally approached her, grabbing her arm, asking her name and *could he give her a kiss?* That was enough to send her running back home, throwing the remaining papers into the bushes. Kam's dad had given all the girls special alarms that you could press to give off the most awful shriek to scare off would-be muggers and murderers.

But her mum had said, "No more papers!" and that Melanie could start applying for proper Saturday jobs in the town. One of the high streets with all the discount shops and the cool record store at the end had a burger place that was hiring younger ones. Melanie wasn't keen at first but her mum had insisted.

"Pel Mel… if you want extra things like the magazine you always have me buy or some sweets at the weekend, it's going to come out of your own money from now on."

Having Dad leave sucked in about fifty-million different ways. And thoughts of Kam went out of her mind as her visits to the shop lessened and it was usually his sister working the till. And then of course, moving again.

Melanie knew that when her dad was around, they didn't need to worry about paying bills, buying new clothes or eating food that actually tasted of something. He had a pretty decent job, something to do with computers and he had to commute an hour and a half to get to it, but it certainly enabled her mother to have weekly shopping trips in town and buy presents for Melanie and Saul. It was all different now.

Melanie's dad kept asking the doctor to sign him off work and she soon noticed that he was always there when she got home from school. Sometimes, she'd ask him to come and hang out and play music but he'd just keep staring ahead, as if waiting for something. She'd shrug and go to her room or go and play Volcano with Saul but it really hurt. Money must have got really tight for them as the next thing she knew, their home was up for sale and they went on the council list, going through a few homes that got progressively worse each time, paint always peeling off the doors and the houses always smelling slightly damp.

Then they finally moved here *when it all happened.*

"It's nearer to where Dad is," her mum had said as if they'd made a great business decision. "And I hear that Chiltern High is one of the best schools in the county. The kids even wear blazers!"

Melanie didn't know how her mum had afforded to buy her the new blazer but was told, "You'll have to make do right now Pel Mel… this is going to have to last you until you leave the school."

When it all happened.

It wasn't just a single event though was it, thought Melanie bitterly. *It had been building up since before I was even born, probably, like the kettle that starts its low whistle and then finally screams for someone to take it off the hob before it explodes. It's probably a God-send that I don't have any mates. I would never want them coming round here.* She picked up her biro and began to write again.

It's the night before I go to Sunny Well… literally cannot believe I can go. Not that I wanted to go there (no thanks to THE LIBRARY!) but at least I'll be out of school! I am half-looking forward to it (no school for two weeks) and half-dreading it (Rachel Shill). I can't BELIEVE that Wrenton put us in the same place and here I was thinking she was a half-decent one. I can hear mum downstairs with Saul, reading a story to him as usual. I love my brother but I wish we were… closer? More like friends? I feel like I am his carer, not his sister sometimes. Mum had a right go at me this morning because I didn't help out at breakfast. What is WITH her at the moment?

I have never seen her so tetchy, not even when Dad was having one of his episodes. I needed a lie-in. How was I supposed to know that she'd been up all night with Saul? He'd wet the bed again... maybe I'll have to deal with that kind of thing at the old people's home, sorry, residential home.

Well, school pretty much sucked as usual this week apart from not having to stand up in front of everyone and apologising – THANK GOD. Rachel kept looking at me in weird ways all week and I swear she made the death sign at me on Tuesday. Maybe she just had an itchy neck. I'll find out at some point I'm sure. Why does she hate me so much? I haven't said so much as one word to her since I started at that school. Anyway, the highlight of the week for me was (drum roll please) not having to go to Mr Roody's room! He is so hideous. Another highlight is that I might be moved up a set in English. I am fed up of being in bottom set. I was never bottom at my old school. As you can see, I am pretty good at writing! OK, I feel it's time dear Diary... for the lowdown! I can't stop thinking about Tim!!!!

Quick Fact File on TIM JONES

Height – Taller than me (I know this because he paused to talk to Candice when we were standing in the hall. He had his back to me but what the hey. He smells pretty good, like aftershave and detergent.

Hair colour – Dark brown (and curly)

Eyes – Haven't got close enough to see... maybe one brown, one green? I like different!!!

Smile – To die for

Does he know I exist? – Certain that he doesn't

Age – Must be same as me or slightly older? Younger? He is in a different house at school but we share a few classes....

Swooooon

Did he see me looking at him at lunch today? – Not sure but one of his friends scowled at me

Fancy my chances? – 7 per cent out of 1000. Ok make that 1 per cent

I wonder if there'll be any decent guys at Sunny

Well? Apparently I will have to wear a uniform! It's green!?!!! And I have to wear black shoes and white ankle socks. I thought I'd get away with wearing jeans and a t-shirt... hang on, Mum's calling (well, shouting actually... seriously!)

Yep, I am supposed to turn my light off and go to bed now. It's only nine! I am FIFTEEN MUM, not seven. I miss Dad at the moment. I can just imagine him in a cell, in a room with no windows or light. Of course I know that is not at all what it will be like in there... but that's all I can see. I miss him SO much. Sometimes I have a picture in my mind of a giant planet earth and we're all on it, except my dad is floating away from it in outer space, all alone with not even a space suit and helmet to protect him. Anyway, where was I... oh yes, Tim Jones!!!! When I look close up at myself in the mirror I think I'm alright – I think my eyes are my best features. If only Tim could get close enough to see them... ARGHHHHH why does my stomach feel like it's in knots? And how can I get rid of these damn spots? Ooh I am a poet and I don't even know it! (bad joke I know!)

There goes mum again shouting her head off. What is WITH you mum! Maybe she's going through 'the change'... we talked about that at school last week. If that is the case, we're in for a bumpy ride. I just feel SO bad for Saul. I am going to start spending more time with him. Anyway, must do night-time routine now (brush teeth, take off make-up etc etc ad nauseam. Still don't know exactly what that expression means but I keep hearing people say it and it sounds kinda cool.) I can hear noises next door. These walls are like paper. When should I call the police? I am surprised they never call them on us with all the shouting that goes on in here at the moment. Goodnight – will write more tomorrow.

ps Dad... if you can hear my thoughts right now...

sometimes, I wish you would just not exist... and that you would also just come home. Not having you here feels like you are dead sometimes. I miss you. I miss your smile and the way you always listened to me moaning on. I miss you reading to Saul so I can spend more time with mum. I miss you putting on your records and dancing like a hippie. Love you. Hate you.

But mainly, love you.

pps I am dreading tomorrow. I am trying to be a teeny tiny bit positive but it's the last place I want to go.

Melanie sighed and felt an ache in her chest. She started to breathe in for ten counts through her nose and then out again. Repeat five times. Everything felt so out of balance. She opened her bottle of olive oil on auto-pilot and swigged it onto fluffy marshmallow cotton wool clouds to remove the black liner and mascara that encircled her eyes. She mimicked her mum in the mirror.

"It's cheaper PEL MEL than real face cream... and better for your skin!"

It was a daily occurrence that one of the lads from the lower sixth muttered within ear-shot 'dodgy goth' but nothing in the world would stop her from wearing eyeliner.

She thought about going to Sunny Well. She had

wanted to talk to Mrs Wrenton all week about Rachel being on the list but could never bring herself to do so. She recalled the time when she was getting changed for PE. She had been in only her underwear and Rachel had given a low whistle then raised her eyebrows.

"*Someone's* been talking to Anna," she'd said loudly and a few other girls had perked their heads up to listen. Melanie had no idea what she was talking about. "Looks like Miss Stoakes has been getting tips for skinny girls... am I right, Mel?" Rachel had looked her up and down and smirked.

Melanie had looked down at her own body half expecting to see something out of place, like a third nipple or a massive hairy mole. She hated the fact they had to get dressed in front of each other and even shower naked. She knew her ribs were visible and she always tried to keep her eyes down but couldn't help but sneak glances at the other girls' bodies. So different from hers. So weird. But surely Rachel wasn't suggesting in her twisted way that she was starving herself? She'd eat everything in sight if she could but there was never anything half-decent in the house. Mainly packs of dried lentils, rice and porridge oats.

Luckily at that point, Miss Garner, the feisty straight-talking PE teacher had come in and blown her whistle loudly. "Two minutes, girls," she'd hollered. She'd clicked the play button on a portable stereo and Jeff Wayne's War of the Worlds started blaring at them all. This was their cue to get a move on. She had fixed her stare on Rachel, speaking louder over the orchestra.

"Stop larking around everyone and that includes you Miss Shill."

There were several stifled giggles when she said the word 'larking'. Rachel had grimaced and continued to pull up her gym socks slowly. She had every teacher on her side… apart from the very astute Miss Garner. When she finally left the room, Rachel quickly came up beside Melanie and whispered, "Don't blow over in the wind, *Anna*."

Oh I get it, Melanie had thought… *very clever! Anna? Anorexic? Wow, that Rachel was a scream.* But as she looked at herself in the mirror, she saw black shadows under her eyes and she scrubbed with the cotton wool, thinking that maybe her make-up hadn't quite come off yet. The dark circles remained.

CHAPTER 8

RACHEL

"MUM! DAD?" Rachel hollered as loudly as she could but she knew they weren't home yet. Their neighbour, Sam, was in the house as usual, minding the dog and doing general cleaning. He was pretty old, in his late seventies, she guessed. *His hair is too long for an old man,* she thought. *Look at how it touches his shoulders at the front and reaches even further down his back. It's like he's time-travelled here from the 1700s. He always smells of some kind of funny tea, smoke and joss sticks. Literally, YUK!* Sam wore hiking sandals with socks when he was in the house then would slip on big black boots to go and walk the dog. He was the opposite of the type of person her mum would allow into their home which meant she had probably taken pity on him.

He looked like he might have been pretty striking at some point in his life but the lines etched on his face and sagging jowls made Rachel feel a bit sick. He brightened up when she walked in but she made a face and grabbed some biscuits from the jar in the kitchen, jumped up on the countertop and banged her feet against the cupboards on purpose as she knew it annoyed him.

"I just cleaned those," Sam muttered and added "… and your mother won't thank you for putting your big clodhoppers on them!"

Rachel turned towards him and tried to make her voice sound older than she was. "Sam, remember that I *live* here… and you come in and walk our dog and clean our house. Now get lost, OK?"

Sam smiled, chuckling a little, pretending that the banter was enjoyable. Rachel knew she was being mean but couldn't help it. He really grossed her out. Once, he'd said, "You have a really slim-line nose, almost like a ski slope but so beautiful. Reminds me of a model I used to date."

She really didn't like Sam being here. He always looked at her when he thought she wasn't paying attention but Rachel always noticed. She could feel his gaze burning into her back.

"Ok, I'll be off then now!" said Sam, a bit too cheerily.

"Ugh, just go home will you? I am not joking!" said Rachel quietly so he couldn't quite make out what she was saying and she sighed loudly and banged her feet louder. He jumped and walked out of the door, still muttering and shaking his head. "What a freak!" she said to the empty house.

Rachel slid off the counter and walked casually into the lounge to enjoy what might be the only down-time she'd have that evening. She put on the TV for a while and soon got bored flicking through the channels. She was one of the few girls in her class who'd had cable installed and at first, she'd been excited to show off her knowledge at school about the new American programmes she had watched like Green Acres, Mr Ed and MTV shows, all things you couldn't get on the usual five channels.

"Boring!" she announced and went upstairs to her parents' bedroom, looking through their drawers. She was never quite sure what she would find but she always rummaged around when they weren't in the house. She felt that they were hiding something from her. Sometimes she'd find a spare bit of money and once a letter from her mum to an old boyfriend in her scarf drawer. It was almost a buzz for her to sneak around, a bit like a spy, to feel the sense of danger and excitement.

Moments later she heard a key in the front door so she jumped up and sloped into her own room as she had done several hundred times before. She could hear her parents' voices and they were arguing as they always did these days, or rather her mum was going on and on in unmerciful tones to her dad. Rachel put on her headphones and looked in the mirror. Her hair clip was beginning to slide down a bit so she re-fastened it and started to apply some lipstick, practising pouting in the mirror. She was told a hundred times a day that she was pretty, sometimes with words but mainly with stolen lustful looks. She hated it. She also loved the attention. But it didn't make her feel any more attractive. She had tonnes of homework but she wanted to make this moment last. The music pounded straight into her ears, just how she liked it, heavy rock, drums beating hard and guitars swaying effortlessly like gliding on clouds, soaring through skies, their solos searing into her heart like golden threads so that she felt connected to the entire universe. She'd just started listening to some new bands from America. She revelled at feeling lost for a few brief moments. She knew her mum would be calling her so she listened for a moment longer, then resigned her headphones to her desk.

"*Rachel,* come down NOW please!" shouted her mum, sounding desperate, having clearly repeated herself several times. Groaning, she trudged downstairs, ready to hear the daily nagging that was about to ensue.

"You still have your boots on Rachel… did you talk to Sam? He didn't look so happy when we saw him just now? Also, do you know that I checked the bathroom this morning and you hadn't flushed *or* covered your sanitary products in the bin?"

Rachel recoiled at her mum's openness in front of her dad, who managed to avoid his daughter's gaze and roll his eyes simultaneously and retreated to his own tiny private study which was *one hundred per cent out of bounds for anyone to enter*. Rachel knew what he had in there: a few packets of cigarettes and two birds in a cage which she hated looking at as it made her feel trapped and shouldn't birds be flying in the sky? There were also a few train magazines and a beautiful box, locked, that she wished belonged to her. She'd had a couple of attempts to find a key but no luck. Her dad had left a cigarette burning once and she'd had a puff. Disgusting! No wonder his breath always smelt terrible.

"And another thing," her mum continued. "This weekend is *definitely* going to be about chores as well as school work. You haven't done much to help around the house this week and Sam is not a professional cleaner, you know that? I wonder if sometimes you are deliberately trying to annoy me Rachel or if you just want me to get upset?"

"Mum!" said Rachel a bit louder than she had anticipated. "Can you please just stop with the moaning?" There was a silence as Rachel's mother looked taken aback. She continued.

"You need to empty your bins and get your homework done...don't forget you have classes all weekend Rachel. You have your Advanced Maths course Saturday morning and Speech and Drama Class from 2pm until 5pm... you need to..."

Rachel stomped up into her room, inwardly chanting 'need-to, need-to' with each step, her hands over her ears. She felt her hair was starting to slide down a little on one side and twisted her fingers around a few strands, marvelling at how real it felt, just like her old hair. She still couldn't quite get used to wearing a wig. She tore it off as it was starting to itch and threw it onto her bed, looking blankly at the beautiful silky raven-black locks that probably used to belong to some girl who could grow her hair over and over again.

"Your hair will probably grow back," the consultant had told Rachel, "but it also might not. We cannot guarantee anything. Each person's experience can be completely different. Be prepared for a life with or without hair. Don't make it identify you. Don't make it *define* you."

But it kind of did when you were a fifteen year-old girl. Losing her hair had been bad but not as downright awful as the daily nagging from her mum. It was relentless. Rachel looked into the mirror and placed her hands onto her crown and felt the smoothness of her head. Like a newborn baby. A hairless baby. She had actually been born with a shock of black hair. She knew this as her mother had told nearly every person she knew, like she just couldn't help herself. And now? She smudged off her eyebrows and took off the fake eyelashes.

Wow, you are one ugly cow Rachel Shill, she thought. *Ugly, ugly, ugly!*

She kept repeating this mantra in her mind and didn't even see her mum come into the room, who for one moment, looked aghast as if she realised for the first time that her daughter was bald. *This is the pattern* thought Rachel. *A repeating pattern of my life. When will it change?* Rachel, as she always did, sat down on the bed, then brought her mother's head towards her as she would a child. Her mother's salty silent tears fell onto her lap as she smoothed her hair and said over and over again, "It's OK mum, please don't cry… it's gonna be OK."

CHAPTER 9

JOHN

John Roody sat on a rickety chair in his back garden, nursing a cup of instant coffee. He was thinking about his life and wondering where it had all gone wrong. When he was a young lad, John was teased mercilessly for having a name like Roody. It wasn't much better now except it just happened to be from a group of wretched pupils behind his back. John wasn't entirely sure how he ended up being a headteacher. It had been a whirlwind decision and not made entirely by himself. He hadn't done so well academically at school, focusing more on being the class clown, making fun of others and trying to divert his peers' attention from the fact that one of his legs was much shorter than the other. This had been the case since birth and he'd undergone several extensive and difficult surgeries as a child including removing two toes on his left foot. He'd blocked out most of the memories but a daily reminder was there in his limp and the fact he had to buy two pairs of shoes each time in two different sizes.

He remembered the day, as a young boy, a bunch of kids from down the street knocking on his door. His dad had opened it, one of the few times he'd been there, and John had stood behind him, looking hopeful that they were going to ask him to come and play. One of the taller lads had been pushed to the front, his face bright red, bits of grass stuck in his hair like he'd been rolling about in a field.

"Hello Sir…" he'd stammered. "Is it true your son's only got three toes on one of his feet?"

All the children had giggled and tried to leg it but he remembered that his dad had walloped that kid into next Sunday then stomped back into the house, his face thunderous, shutting himself in his study with not a single look at his son. He didn't come out until his mother had returned from her daily grocery shopping trip. His mum always had the right way with his dad, always knew how to bring him back from one of his foul moods.

But the most painful memory was when his mother announced,

"John… it's time you swallowed your pride and put these on!"

She'd thrust into his arms a pair of clunky black boots to make his legs evenly matched in height which in turn would improve his gait and general bone structure in his back.

"I hate them!" he'd howled. "They're so heavy… and they pinch! Mother, I really do hate them… look at how they make me walk. The lads at school are going to rag on me for this… they'll call me retarded Mother, do you realise?"

"Don't use that word, John Roody! Now just put them on and be done with it. You'll be glad you did when you're older."

The snide comments and jeers were thrown at him from the get-go and he'd laughed it off on the outside whilst inwardly seething.

"Don't you dare let their words get to you John Roody," his mother would say, hugging him tightly until he could hardly breathe. "Don't let them see you upset. Put on a brave face, my strong man. Dry those tears and walk out of here this morning with your back straight and your walk purposeful."

Her words however didn't stop the taunts of "Gammy Leg, Gammy Peg, if I were you then I'd be dead!"

John had considered most of his class half-wits but there were a few decent eggs in there like Michael McCreedy and Simon Manners.

"Aw, just ignore them, Roody," they'd say, whilst inhaling the smoke wafting out of the teachers' lounge as deep into their lungs as possible. They gained great satisfaction from spying on the teachers at break, sneaking cigarettes from Mr Spears, the geography teacher and a puff of his pipe on Friday afternoons when instead of teaching about maps and rivers, he'd pop his feet up on the desk, smoking away whilst the lads threw paper around the classroom and drew pictures of girls they fancied. They even managed to get a drop of whisky once when Michael's dad died. It all made their lives at school a little more exciting. They formed a strong bond and made a pact by spitting on their hands and rubbing them together. They got into trouble most days, often taking the rap for one another and it was not uncommon for them to be called to the headmaster's room for a belt across the back of the legs, except Roody always got it on his hands.

Getting married was a big surprise for John but Denise Walker had a thing for him at university, where he attended as a mature student, trying to obtain for a second time the degree he knew his father really wanted him to have.

"You don't want to waste your life like the other lads are doing," his dad would say, a record stuck on repeat. "You did rubbish at school, mucking around and playing the fool… what are you doing to do with your life? When are you going to get that nose to the grindstone, eh?"

His father was often very hard on him. He spoke harsh, mean words but never ever laid a finger on him which was half the trouble really. No beltings or sticks on the leg as his mates often got but also no hugs, not even a playful ruffle of the hair. It was as if he was completely infatuated with only John's mother and had no room for anything or anyone else.

Which is why it surprised John, when his own daughter was born, that his dad fell in love, completely besotted! His dad doted on his new baby granddaughter, making John feel resentful rather than happy. Where was all this love when he was a child? He couldn't help but make the comparison.

Getting divorced was a less of a surprise. John would look at Denise, incredulous, as she'd say the most horrible words to him and it would make him feel like a child again, standing behind his dad at the front door.

"You're not the same man I married, John. You don't do a thing to help me at home… when are you going to get a proper job? While all my friends are getting the latest designer purses, handbags and going on holidays, I'm stuck here with my bleeding shopping trolley. *Be a man John… go and get a real job!*"

Eventually John began to feel different about Denise. He knew he'd changed too. Their daughter was often caught in the middle of their battles and it wasn't long before she started siding with her mother, also telling him what a letdown for a dad he was. Having the words, "I hate you!" thrown in his face was a common occurrence in their house-hold. He even began he hate himself. He soured over the years and started to get annoyed by everything. He wanted to make it work but Denise felt trapped by their relationship and didn't seem to get on with his parents. She always had something mean-spirited to say about them, even his mother, who was the most caring and generous person he'd ever met.

"Your mum!" Denise had once spat at the dinner table. "She gave me a right look last week when they visited and I said I wanted to get a new conservatory. They look down on me John, I know it. I won't stand for it here, I just won't."

They had, of course, argued heavily as John tried to defend his mother's honour. "There's not a single bad bone in her body!" he'd seethed. "*It's not on Denise* that you speak about her this way."

It was only a matter of time before his parents stopped visiting as much. There had been one final awful time which ended in Denise screaming at his dad. And then that was it. She met a bloke from up north and she and his daughter were gone in a flash.

John's friend, Gary, had worked at the local council offices and he'd seen an opening for a headteacher's position at the local comprehensive.

"Look," Gary had said to John over a beer and a game of snooker. "Your divorce has finally come through and you don't even see your daughter anymore..."

"Well, except our awfully awkward yearly visits where I stay in some murky downtown hotel near my ex-wife and see my daughter for about two hours a day," John had grumbled.

Or sometimes she'd come to him, spending hours on a coach, arriving late at night and spending most of the visit not talking to him. It never went well. And now, he didn't even have a proper hobby to keep him occupied so he was going out of his mind with boredom, not to mention needing the money.

"They're really desperate," his friend had advised. "It's a non-teaching position, just all admin and behaviour management. You'd be great at it John. I know things have been tough, really tough, since your ex... well, since she lied about you so she could get custody. Maybe whilst you let things settle, you could think about it? Might take your mind off it... even a bit of a welcome distraction?"

No-one else, it seemed, had wanted to apply for the job so John had won it hands down. The best thing about the new role was the rather grand room he could work from, which he saw as a haven away from the rest of the school. Proper mahogany desk, luxury chair and even his own personal coffee-maker. He had to call weekly staff-meetings which he detested and he knew his colleagues didn't think much of him. He couldn't quite recall when he started to get so angry about things.

It was maybe around the same time that his daughter had turned eleven and had written a short, impersonal letter.

Dear Dad,

Life in Scotland is good. Everyone is well. I spoke to Mum and it's going to be hard to keep coming to visit. I will be putting all my focus on school work now. Sorry Dad... the journey's too far and it's difficult for me. I do love you but I want to stay here with Mum and make sure my grades are good.

ps I got a new hamster. His name is Laika, like the first dog who was in space. I know it's not a dog... but you know mum and her allergies.

John sighed and tipped his now cold coffee into the bushes in the garden. He couldn't figure out why every single thing was messed up. He pretended not to care but it all kept hitting him like punches to the stomach. That letter from his daughter! It was like Denise had been standing over his daughter whilst she wrote it. It reeked of her. He missed his daughter so much and he'd let her go without a fight. His ex had managed to really dig into the depths of depravity and pulled out so many lies. It was like all the life he had in him was starting to just disperse into a nothing. *He was becoming nothing.* It was seeping into every part of his world and swallowing him up whole. He didn't see his dad anymore and his beloved mother had died. "I've got a school where I don't want to work, my desk, my coffeemaker and those blasted pupils." John said bitterly. "That's all I've got!"

CHAPTER 10

MELANIE

Melanie awoke to the sound of the radio playing some terrible yet catchy pop song rising from the kitchen and could hear her mum singing at the top of her voice. *Odd,* she thought. *That never happens. Well, it used to but not since Dad left.*

She was glad though as it was good to get up early today. She was dreading going to Sunny Well but also felt strangely intrigued and she definitely didn't want to miss the mini-bus. Rachel lived near her estate but in a much nicer area called Golden Ash – new builds with front porches, pebble-dash pavements, brand new yellow silt boxes, complete with council logo and not even a spray of graffiti. It was only a short walk away but the kids over there always looked down on the likes of this part of town. She wondered who'd be picked up first, hoping it would be her so she could sit right at the back and blend into her seat without any obvious awkwardness.

Like a robot on automatic, she slumped her body out of

bed, splashed water on her face, clicked *play* on the stereo, then started to apply the concealer that would at least reduce the redness of some of the pox scars. Kate Bush started to wail about the wily, windy moors as Melanie dipped into her beauty box from her thirteenth birthday (that had been a surprise, getting that from her mum) and found her most prized possession, a black kohl pencil. She started to go through the motions of her daily ritual, applying an arch of black eyeliner, sweeping past her eyebrows and curling into a spiral at the end, gracing her already long lashes with thick, black mascara and then a faint black line, outlining her lips, ensuring the cupid's bow was deftly considered.

Her body moved the whole time to the music. The higher the pitch, the more shivers would run up and down her spine. She felt the music was inside of her body, pulsating through her blood and veins. She immediately rubbed off the lip definition. *Too much* she mused. *I don't want to scare off the old biddies.* She imagined Tim looking at her from the mirror. She felt her belly flip a little and her heart started to pick up speed. Maybe they could listen to records together instead of her and Dad.

Flash of guilt. Sick to the stomach.

She could hear sounds from the kitchen and the smell of sizzling animal flesh wafted up the stairs. Surely Mum hadn't give into Saul's demands for bacon?

As she continued to add colour to her cheeks and run a brush through her hair, attempting a French plait, she thought back to a time when she had been small, not sure of the age but little enough to have been carried on her dad's shoulders. It must have been on one of his good days as she remembered his face wreathed in smiles. They were looking at a jigsaw in a shop window in the store in town, the one with the toy monkey on the swing that kept heaving itself over its bar, grinning madly at all the children. She'd marvelled at the jigsaw picture, a summer scene with butterflies fluttering, without a care, through a cornflower blue sky. She had pointed and asked her dad for one.

Later that day, when he'd opened the box for her, Melanie had been disappointed to see that the picture was in little pieces.

"Daddy!" she'd wailed. "Where did the pretty picture go?" She'd cried and ran to her room. Saul had joined her and they'd bawled loudly together even though he was not sure what they were crying about.

"Hey Mel... come here," her dad had said. "You take this piece... and fit it... right here...to this other piece! You've got to keep looking for the right bits and then finally, you'll have your butterflies back again."

She'd whined that she really wanted it on her wall so

he'd glued the pieces together, made a little frame and hung it above her desk.

When he left, she'd broken it to pieces, angry and confused as to why he'd gone, so suddenly, with no real explanation. Her mum had found it in the bin and said matter-of-factly,

"It's just us three now Pel Mel, for the time being. He'll come back… he just needs time."

How much time? Why couldn't anyone say?

Melanie had felt like the broken jigsaw in the trash and had thought, *what if I want to just clear off? Can I? How would the pieces of our family fit back together if one piece was permanently missing?*

Melanie tutted as she realised she'd messed up the plait. She really needed a hair-cut. "Today's the day Pel Mel," she said to herself in the mirror. "Are you ready for those golden oldies and to hang out with your best friend in the whole-wide world, Rachel Shill?"

She'd moaned a lot to her mum the previous evening about spending two whole weeks with her 'arch-enemy' but Angela had brushed it off, as she shook towels and bedsheets and pushed two corners of a blanket into Melanie's hands so she could help to fold them.

"Melanie… I know that I'm not always so positive. I work hard… it's tough for me too you know? I want the best for you and Saul. For Pete's sake, your dad's no help at the moment where he is. Sometimes I feel I could do with a break and join him. But you know what? I'm doing this on my own. We don't know when Dad's going to come out. I want to say he will and I believe he will get better but I don't know that and I don't want to lie to you. Now, you can flipping well manage two weeks working with someone you don't like and in a place that wasn't your first choice. You never know. You might actually learn something new. Things are not always what they seem. Maybe give this Rachel girl a chance?"

The look on her face and the fact she'd called her *Melanie,* meant that answering back had not been an option. *What about all the dirty looks I get from Rachel, every single day at school? Give her a chance? Fat lot of good that would do.*

Melanie took one last look in the mirror then went downstairs and sat at the table. There was porridge with raisins, a plate of bacon in the middle and a bunch of dandelions in a tiny cup. *Weeds are flowers* her mum would say.

"Bacon was on offer," her mum said with a smile and continued to set the table, clinking glasses for juice and setting out the margarine and toast. Melanie noticed she was wearing a new top and even had a touch of make-up on. She looked pretty. "Come on Pel Mel. Serve yourself!

You're going to need a good meal this morning to keep your energy up!"

"Mel... are you coming back, or are you leaving like Dad?" asked Saul, his mouth crammed full of bacon, juice dripping down his chin. Melanie wiped him with his own sleeve, took three rashers for herself and started to spread her toast.

"Saul... I already told you, I'm going to work at the old people's home. You know, I might have to wipe their butts!" Saul snorted juice out of his nose.

"MUM! She said *butts!*"

"I don't know which jobs I'll be given but you know what? Maybe it'll be OK." Melanie glanced quickly at her mum. "Maybe, just a little bit, I'm looking forward to it. Who knows? It might just be something I want to do when I leave school. I mean, I doubt it! I reckon I'll have enough of the old fogeys after a few days! Oh no, it's going to smell gross in there! Anyway... come here Saul! Just for the record... of course I am coming back. Love ya!" Melanie punched his arm playfully and then they all heard a loud beep outside which meant her ride was here.

"Looks like they picked up your friend first," said her mum glancing out of the window. "Here, put your breakfast in a Tupperware and take it with you."

Melanie looked up and saw Rachel leaning on the

window, her breath steaming up the glass. She didn't look so happy or awake. She frowned at her mum, suddenly wishing that she could just stay at home. "She's not my friend, mum," Melanie breathed in deeply and swallowed her panic. "But yeah… I'll give it a go."

CHAPTER 11

SALLY

Sally waited impatiently by the front door, reading a tattered old poster about funeral homes. She wondered who on earth had put it there. Finally, she saw the mini-bus and started to wave although no-one was looking her way. She watched as two forlorn girls got off the bus and made their way across the car park, not smiling, not looking up, not talking. *Well, this is going to be fun,* Sally thought. *What a pair of young misery guts they've sent to us!*

"Welcome to Sunny Well!" Sally enthused as much as she could and laughed to herself as it sounded like she was welcoming them to a summer holiday camp. "So… let me guess! Rachel?" Sally looked at Melanie, who shook her head. "Oops!" remarked Sally. "Well, it's nice to meet you both! You're going to have a great time here… it really depends on how much you put in as to how much you'll get out. Just breathe and keep calm!"

Hark at me, Sally thought. *I sound like a wacky guru! I'll be burning some incense soon and wafting sage around these two. Never seen such surly faces.*

"Right, well, follow me and we'll get you meeting and greeting everyone."

Sally led them around the home, pointing out where they could eat lunch, take a break and introducing them to some of the residents. She thought that Melanie had a bit more of a spark about her whilst Rachel looked positively horrified when one of the residents started to moan about her Weetabix and threw spoonfuls of mushy wheat on the floor.

"We'll sort that out, never mind," said Sally briskly. "Right! So, Rachel… I think I'm going to give you some folding to do today. Now, don't look quite so worried! It's boring work but it's necessary and it will give the other girls a bit of a break. It's also super easy! Do you think you can manage to do that?"

Rachel grimaced and nodded and Sally looked at the two of them, wondering if perhaps she should send them both back to the mini-bus.

"So Rachel, dear," Sally continued, trying her best to jolly the girls along, glancing over the rim of her spectacles, smiling broadly. "I'll show you where all the sheets and blankets are, plus the bigger towels, the hand towels, the face flannels, the linen and…"

Sally continued to reel off a long list of the folding

needs of the home whilst Rachel glowered at Melanie.

"OK, get to it, then! Just down the corridor and open the cupboard on the left. You'll see the clean linen in there, which should get you started. None of it is folded, which is where you come in!"

Rachel clumped down the hallway in her big boots and suddenly it was just Melanie and Sally alone in the corridor. Sally took a breath and looked serious. She kept this facial expression for moments when she wanted to have an effect on someone.

"So, Melanie, let me ask you one thing. When you leave here, what do you want to have achieved?"

They spoke right outside George's door about how Melanie helped care for her brother at home and she even started to talk a bit about her dad.

"So you see, Miss Sally…" continued Melanie.

"Oh pet, just call me Sally please! No need for formality here. The other girls will laugh at you!"

Sally tried to figure Melanie out. She definitely had a way about her. She reminded her a bit of herself. Melanie cleared her throat and continued.

"I guess… well… I guess I don't really know. My mum always says that, er… my dad… well, he's in a sort of home… hospital. I dunno. He told my mum he doesn't want visitors while he… um… gets better but I always hope that someone who works there is checking in on him every day. I hope that he's not lonely in there. Do you know what I mean? I didn't really want to come here if I'm honest. I know that sounds bad and I don't mean to sound ungrateful or anything. I think if there's anyone I can help whilst I'm here? Maybe I could just do that? Check in on someone? I've never done anything like this before. I love writing and I wanted to work in the library… but oh, I can fold clothes and towels… if you need me to…"

Sally smiled at Melanie. "I like you!" she said. "You're a good egg! I love your honesty. So nice to hear someone your age saying it like it is! You like writing, you say? I think I know just the person for you. He's grumpy, mind you… and he's got Alzheimer's. Early stages. And other problems too. I'll tell you all about George and we'll see how you get on OK? You'll be fine here, love. Just ask me if you need anything."

Sally knocked on George's door. "George!" she called out.

"You've got a visitor!"

CHAPTER 12
GEORGE

George could hear noises outside his room. He sat on his bed, head lowered, eyes cast down, tears falling softly, silently onto the carpet. He wasn't sure why he was crying. He'd had his lunch already. Ham sandwiches as it always was on a Monday. Or was it breakfast that he'd eaten? He couldn't remember. He thought that one of the staff members had spoken rudely to him earlier so he'd raised his voice at her and said some cutting words. She had quickly scurried away and the next thing he knew, the line manager of Sunny Well had come to check he was OK.

"Everyone treats me like a baby," he'd lamented. "I just want to be left alone."

But when he was alone, he'd sometimes hear the ticking of the clock and the birds outside and long to be in nature, in the fresh air. But his thoughts always persisted, telling him things he didn't want to hear.

You're no good. You have failed at life.

No-one comes to see you George because you're not lovable.

Your own family don't even want to know you. What does that say about you, eh?

He'd practically lived in the outdoors as a child, always running free and soaking up the rays of the sun, standing with his arms outstretched, his tongue out as far as it would go to catch the rain and rolling the biggest snowballs to make giant snowmen in winter. Every time he thought about going out now, the walls of the room seemed to move inwards. It had been too long.

He could sometimes hear voices in his room and he would talk back to them. They would ask, "Are you going on your boat this fine morning, George? Where will you be sailing to today?"

He had always wanted to go to China. Maybe his boat could sail him there? He hoped he'd remember how to steer. He knew enough to not tell anyone about the voices. He tuned into the noise outside in the hallway and realised it was two people having a conversation.

He pressed his ear against the door straining to decipher who it was. Sally was definitely one of the people. He would recognise her soft tones in any crowd. And someone else? She sounded young. He heard his name being mentioned a few times and felt a deep flush in his cheeks as if he'd been caught doing something he shouldn't. He was starting to worry a lot more these days and kept trying to remember places, people and times in his life that were important but they became increasingly blurred. He went to his desk to make sure the ceramic kitten was where he'd left it.

"You're the centre of my universe you are," he said, finding the cold, smooth feel of the kitten comforting. As he turned it round in his hand, he started to have thoughts that he knew he really wanted to hold onto.

There was this one time he had been running through a big field away from a tree. He used to know all the names of the trees where he lived but this one seemed to linger just under his tongue, not allowing him to form the word. He was being chased by something and had to get away. What was it? He was sure that his best friend Jimmy had been with him. He closed his eyes and searched his mind. He could smell summer, long grass, heat and sweat. There was a wheat-cutter in the next field, and men were shouting to each other. He thought he could hear the ocean too but that couldn't have been right as there was no sea for miles. He smiled as flickers of the memory came to him like waves, bringing more to the scene each time.

"Ah yes," he said and paused. "Yes… Jimmy, you were there! And it was the most beautiful summer's day. We had been out looking for wood to carve and had stumbled across a tree with a hive in it. Oh we were so foolish,

Jimmy! If we hadn't thrown the stones, the bees wouldn't have been so angry with us!"

George remembered running and then suddenly realising that it was futile. He had been told by his great-aunt, who also kept bees in her beautiful forest garden, with wild flowers weaving and winding through the tufts of turf, to keep still and breathe slowly, relax and feel at peace when around these creatures. He'd stood in the field, his arms outstretched, eyes closed, face tilted slightly to the sun and steadying his racing heart-beat. The bees had settled on him, covering half his face, arms and torso, vibrating their wings, soft and light. He'd felt like he was humming and buzzing along with them. *He was a bee!* He smiled as he recalled not a single one stung him that day. He'd felt invincible and wildly alive. His friend Jimmy though… George remembered screaming and shouting. Had Jimmy gone to hospital? His mind flickered to another scene. His car reversing backwards and driving over a small pink bike. Again, there had been screaming. He screwed his eyes tight to both forget and remember.

A branch tapping on his window made his memories scatter, like broken glass with shards of each picture shooting back into the depths of his mind. He felt irritated and decided that he would not open his door for anyone today. The voices continued and he pushed it open, just a crack, to see. There was a young girl outside with her back to him and he could see Sally nodding and opening her eyes wide, smiling, cocking her head to one side. The girl's hair was caught in a ray of sunlight that had escaped into the hallway, dust-motes dancing erratically, dipping and diving. Beautiful long copper-coloured hair, like the sand from the beach he used to visit in his youth. He drew in his breath sharply and closed the door. It couldn't be. It was not possible. That young girl he'd just seen. That young lass was Bitsy.

CHAPTER 13
MELANIE

At the end of the first day of work experience, the phone rang. Melanie's mum always wanted someone else to pick up but they never did. After about the thirtieth ring, it stopped.

"PEL MEL!" her mum screeched and Melanie shot downstairs thinking something terrible had happened to Saul. Angela stood in the hallway, tapping her foot, her head angled curiously to one side and giving Melanie the strangest look.

"It's a *boy?*" she mouthed looking equally confused and delighted, handing the lime green receiver over. Melanie held it in her hands. It felt so unfamiliar to her. Panic started to rise from her stomach. Maybe it was Mr Roody and her mum was mistaken. Nobody had her number so perhaps it was actually just a trick. Was it Sally? Did she do something wrong today at the home? OK so Sally wasn't a boy or a man, she knew that but still… who on earth could it be? Her throat started to close and her mind started to fold in on itself as the all too-familiar palpitations started to thump away in her chest. Her mum gestured wildly at the phone impatiently. Melanie took a few deep breaths.

"Hello?"

An equally nervous voice answered. "Hi... er, is this Melanie? Melanie Stoakes? I, er... got your number from the book."

The voice was a little rough and Melanie couldn't for the life of her figure out who it was.

"Who is this?" she demanded, suddenly feeling annoyed that her privacy had been interrupted. She felt sure Rachel had put someone up to calling her. The Someone cleared his throat.

"Er... it's Timothy. Tim. Tim Jones from school? I got your number from the book, just in case... you were, you know..."

Melanie sank down to the floor, her legs feeling like they had actually turned to jelly. They wobbled and shook and she couldn't get them back under control. *I am going to vomit* she thought. *I am going to vomit and Tim Jones, if this is really him, is going to hear me vomit. And that will literally be the end of me.*

"Hi Tim," she said as casually as she could. "What's going on?" She cringed as she heard her words. This was the most she'd said to anyone in ages. Why did she have to sound so lame? And why on God's green earth was Tim Jones of all people calling her? She didn't even know they were listed in the book until he'd told her, twice!

"I just wanted to know what you're doing sometime this week or, I dunno, maybe the weekend?" said Tim sounding a little more confident. "Do you want to, you know… hang out at some point? Maybe we can go to the Rec or something? Just hang out, you know…. like…?"

Was that actually a sentence, Melanie thought and without even trying, she smiled and felt her heart might possibly burst out of her body. He didn't sound at all like she thought he would. She thought his voice would be somewhat… deeper?

"Sure," she said. "What time? I can be there at ten in the morning on Sunday. I've got nothing else better to do," she added hastily.

"OK, ten it is. See you soon, Mel."

And with that, he hung up. He'd called her Mel.

"Pel Mel!" her mum called from upstairs sounding slightly hysterical. "It sounds like you might have someone interested in you!"

Melanie swore under her breath as she realised that her mum had been listening on the other phone and then went straight to her room, grabbed the nearest pen and started to write furiously.

DEAR DIARY‼️ OK... OK! WHAT just happened??!‼️ Honestly... what just happened?! I don't get it. Number one, how on earth did TIM JONES know my second name? And number two... what on EARTH?

Melanie sat at her desk, feeling numb and strange and excited and terrified all at once. She stared up at her reflection in the mirror and tried to remember any encounter she'd had with Tim but couldn't recall a single one apart from one time in class. Had he noticed her? Well, more than she'd realised? She spent most of her time avoiding all eye-contact with anyone at school so it was possible. The more she thought about it, the more she couldn't remember seeing him hang out with anyone at school. He was always in a crowd for sure but usually walking down the hallways going from one class to the next. Was there a time that he'd looked back at her? Or was she just imagining that now and hoping?

She looked at her eyes closely and saw that the black circles had started to fade a little. She'd been sleeping better the last few days and sitting down to eat more with Saul and Mum. The pressure was definitely less now she wasn't at school. Even after one day, she felt like she fitted in at Sunny Well. It was a strange feeling but Sally was like an older sister. It had been a weird and good day. She looked deep into her own eyes and wrote without even looking at the paper.

I like the way my eyes look really close up, the amber-coloured irises with flecks of molten brown making them dance a little. Would Tim like them, I wonder? Like me? I wonder what music he's into... oh God... what if he likes Spandau Ballet? Stop being silly Pel Mel! Tim Jones called YOU. Maybe I should go into the town library and get some tapes... just to brush up on some new music. OK... breathe Mel...

She closed her eyes and placed her fingers on the lines of her cheekbones, stroking them gently, feeling shivers go up and down her spine. Her fingers traced the pimples and scars. Would Tim like those too?

She tried to remember a time when her dad had said anything about her looks. He'd usually call her Pumpkin, Popsicle, Poppadom or other items of food; *My little carrot top, my baby beet';* but nothing of any real consequence. Was that a good thing? Most of the time though, her dad had sat in the green chair in the lounge, his eyes focused on the curtains, his mood heavy and his breathing slow. It was at these times that Melanie would go to her room whilst her mum would bustle about, making tea and acting as if it was completely normal for her husband to stop speaking. Her mum always said she looked beautiful but didn't all mums say that?

What are the chances? So... let me go back to the beginning. Why is TIM JONES, of all people calling me? RACHEL SHILL if you have anything to do with this, I swear...

Melanie glanced back at herself in the mirror and thought about how the first day at Sunny Well had gone. Melanie felt that Sally had warmed to her more than Rachel, which made her feel secretly happy and slightly guilty. She thought it had been hilarious that Rachel had been assigned to folding duties. Melanie had almost laughed out loud when that happened. Her face had been a real picture when Sally had announced this as if it was an amazing job that everyone was hoping for. Melanie felt herself brighten a little and picked up her pen.

I don't know what's happening! They say good things happen in threes. So there's Tim calling me and Sally actually called me SWEET ONE! She said that George had had no visitors for over TWO YEARS! I'd visit my Dad if I was allowed! Strange moment alert!!!! I met 'Old

George' for the first time and he came out of his room and looked at me as if he'd seen a ghost!

It was the weirdest moment of my life and that includes many MANY weird things! Sally was about to introduce me but George suddenly took out a hanky and in it was wrapped a little kitten, like something you'd put on your shelf as an ornament. Then he said something that was even weirder! He called me his 'Dear child' and gave me a hug! Strangely, I didn't feel threatened though. It felt nice and friendly. He then put this little kitten into my hand and said he'd wanted to give this to me for a long time. And then THANKED me for coming to visit!!!!! And then the biggest weird thing happened... he turned to Sally and said, 'Sally! Let me introduce to you... my Bitsy!'

Maybe the third good thing will be that me and Rachel become best friends! Ha! That would be more of a miracle... not blooming likely.

Melanie hugged her knees and felt her world changing ever so slightly. What was it her dad had said once? Something about how you can attract good things into your life when you change your attitude? Or think good thoughts? *Maybe I deserve some nice moments for once* thought Melanie. The reflection in the mirror gave her a little smile. "I deserve nice things!" said Melanie, brightening. "I deserve a friend... or two. I deserve to be happy."

CHAPTER 14
RACHEL

Rachel had been home for a few hours now and no-one had come in yet. Was it Bridge night? Impromptu work-do?

Surely her parents couldn't have gone out on a date?

The first day at Sunny Well had pretty much sucked. Sharing a bus with grumpy, long-faced Melanie was bad enough and then Sally, who fancied herself living in a different era with her strange pink hair had clearly not taken a liking to her.

She'd folded so many towels and sheets that her wrists ached. She talked out loud, her nose wrinkling in disgust.

"What's the point of work experience anyway? I don't want to ever work in a home, that's for sure. It always smells of other people's urine, sweat and over boiled broccoli. I'm fifteen for God's sake! I have no idea what I want to do with my life!"

A memory flashed through Rachel's mind.

"I've signed you up to *Tod Mods!*" her mum had announced one day at breakfast, when Rachel had been young enough to not know how to tie her own laces.

"They take on models up to age seven. Do you want to do that? Look pretty in the pictures? Your face could be all over the town!"

The agency was tucked away in the heart of London and she remembered having to get several buses and tube stops to get there. She'd been in a few catalogues as a toddler and even an advert on TV promoting some kind of kid's yoghurt. But all the waiting around, not getting as many call-backs as the agency hoped for, not to mention how boring the whole process was meant that eventually, they'd turned from modelling to activities. Lots and lots of activities. Her mum just wanted her to be good at every-thing. Every. Single. Thing.

Rachel opened the window in her bedroom and stared out to the back of the garden, watching carefully as the light transformed slowly to dark, the shades and shadows shape-shifting from slow-moving overhanging swollen clouds, waters breaking, giving birth to new born rain. She loved looking out of her window. It was her own space in the busy-ness of life, house and mind. Her head was itching furiously and she knew better than to scratch. She gently unfastened the pink clip; a goodbye present from her best friend Moira at her previous school; and then felt the dreamy feeling of bliss and joy as she took the mass of hair off and hung it on its stand and the sting in her heart, that she never heard from her friend anymore, not since the day she left.

The wig was in dire need of a wash. She had not only folded a particularly large mountain of clothes today at the home, which was surprisingly sweaty work, but she'd hung out with some of the older girls at break and they'd been smoking around her hair. The smoke had woven its way into the fibres, the smell choking and grey. She'd hardly seen Melanie but knew that soon, she might also be asked to make some visits to the residents. Ugh! It turned her stomach to think she might have to touch one of them or even worse, feed them. She much preferred where she was, more behind the scenes.

She looked carefully outside into their neatly formed and perfectly landscaped garden, trimmed and mowed, with every blade of grass in place.

Everything had to be perfect.

She enjoyed watching the objects in the garden become disfigured by the absence of light and colours diffused from reds and greens and blues to patterns of shadows. She longed for the sound of thunder or rain or any diverse weather system which would ruin the garden a little, scattering random leaves and flowers. She wanted it to look more like chaos. Emotions that she'd harnessed for far too long inside started to rise within her body. She wanted to shriek and holler, an enraged banshee, a warrior preparing to go into battle. She wanted to shout at her mother.

Enough! *Enough mother! Just let me be! Let's go back to how it used to be before… before I lost all my hair. I am the same person, Mum!*

But Rachel felt a twist inside her gut as she knew she'd allowed herself to become embittered and impatient. She hadn't meant to be so awful at school but leaving her old life behind was quite possibly the biggest wrench and hardship she'd ever had to face. And that included, what was the official word they had used down the surgery?

Alopecia Universalis.

Total hair loss.

Auntie Joan had come to stay, more for her mum than for her. *That's right* Rachel had thought. *My hair falls out and Mum makes it all about her with a mini-breakdown.* Joan had not uttered a single word of pity but instead got on with teaching her how to make her eyebrows look incredible, better than her old ones even, topping her up on the best quality fake eye-lashes and helping her choose a wig from one of the most reputable shops in London, making jokes that made her feel better, like, "At least you don't have to wax your upper lip now, Rach… it was getting quite hairy up there love!" Rachel had heard Joan speaking to her mum, telling her not to cry and to stop showing all her feelings to her daughter.

"You've got to make sure Rachel still feels like you love her. You do… still love her, right?"

Her mum had shouted, "Of course I do, Joan! But people will think it was my fault! They always look to the mother, don't they! They always, *always* blame the mum!"

They had continued to argue back and forth and after Joan had left, nothing much changed. She could still hear her mum crying herself to sleep each night and her dad spent more and more time in his den. She wished that her aunt had stuck around. She lived miles away overseas teaching children in the rural villages of a place she'd never heard of.

Why couldn't she go and live with her?

Alopecia Universalis.

Sometimes, Rachel would say these two words aloud, letting the words drip off her tongue, a bittersweet mix of honey and a foul-tasting medicine.

She'd received comments about her natural hair since she was tiny, as it used to be so sleek and smooth. Her mum had always made her wear it long. She'd begged for a bobcut when they came out in fashion but her mum had refused.

"It took me years to get your hair looking like this

Rachel… and you look so pretty, darling. Like a beautiful princess!"

They'd replicated her hair perfectly. Perfectly, imperfect. If only people could just notice her for the right reasons. She got noticed at school, she made sure of that. But after every time, she felt the same knotted feeling in her tummy and splinters of stubborn guilt lashing her mind.

She thought of Melanie and almost hissed audibly as she considered how beautiful she was.

"She just sits there, looking so frickin' pretty and perfect and she doesn't even flipping well know it," she said out loud. She always noticed Melanie looking over at them and felt she was being aloof, distancing herself from the girls.

She'd embarrassed herself once when she'd shouted at a young girl on her first day. She didn't want to get bullied like she had at her first secondary school, before her mum uprooted all of them to move here. She wanted to make sure that never happened again in the history of her life. She was not going to be made a victim. She'd said something stupid to Melanie to try and make herself look bigger than she felt. *She couldn't possibly have bought it* Rachel thought. *I'm a terrible actor.*

That day, in her old school, when Jonathan Hamilton came up to her and said out loud in front of everyone, a glint in his eye as if he'd been planning this one for a while, "Hey Rach! You're looking a bit... shiny there! You know, on the top of your head! Might want to get a pen and colour it in!" was when she realised the jig was up. Everyone had laughed, of course, including her but she'd been inwardly horrified.

Jonathan sought every opportunity to humiliate her in front of her friends including shoving a handful of snow in her face one winter which had choked her as she'd felt it go deep into her mouth, tiny stones leaving scratches on her face. That's what you got for turning down Jonathan Hamilton. The boy that everyone fancied. And wouldn't take no for an answer, well not without a fight anyway.

The last straw was when she'd given him one more chance and they'd lain on the grass together at school on one of the hills by the trees at the back where the older kids went to sneak cigarettes and time how long they could hold their breath until they passed out. Jonathan and Rachel both looked up at the sky, just talking and Rachel felt in the moment that just maybe she could actually consider being his proper girlfriend. Sure, he was annoying and behaved like an eight-year old half the time but he had those eyes that made your heart flutter a little and fall a bit in love with him, even when he was being a jerk. He'd ruined the moment in an instant as the next thing she knew, he'd rolled on top of her and started kissing her. He'd pinned her down and the smell of his breath had made her retch. She'd kicked him off furiously and as she'd walked away, seething, she could hear him shooting all manner of profanity her way, demeaning and disgusting words that would form a repeating patten in her head.

There's no-one else that'll go out with you Rach... have you seen yourself lately? You're such a tease.

I'm only taking pity on you. Don't think for one moment that I actually ever liked you!

Good luck Rach... once this gets round school, you'll find yourself with less mates than Miranda Blake.

Her mum, of course, had taken the school down and Jonathan had been asked to leave quietly as a law suit had been threatened. And then before she knew it, just like that, they'd moved schools.

She wondered what had happened to Jonathan. Was he in some other school still pushing himself on other girls that he thought were pretty and weak? She didn't care right now. That was one time she'd seen her mum shown great courage. What on earth had happened now?

Rachel knew that clumps of hair were clogging the shower drain and she'd tried to hide them from her mum, making sure the bathroom door was always locked, rolling it all in tissues and putting them at the bottom of the bin.

Her mum had a habit of barging in at the most inopportune moments like when she was checking her breasts for lumps as her aunt had taught her, as it was *never too early*, or squeezing a stray spot before her mum could notice. *If only she'd stop going on about flipping clubs!* It was one thing after the other! She imitated her mum. "We must fit in, darling! Everyone else is signing their kids up to all these… what are they calling them? *Extra-curricular activities*! And we need to make sure we don't stand out here… or that you don't get left behind!"

Everything in their life was about not standing out, not being different. Her mum couldn't even bear if it Rachel had a blemish on her skin. She kept her daughter on a strict diet of vitamins, fruits, veggies, and proteins plus some herbal remedies and concoctions that smelt and tasted gross.

"But Mum!" Rachel had moaned. "You say you don't want me to stand out then send me to school with a Holly Hobbie lunchbox and quinoa-stuffed peppers, whilst all my mates are filling their faces with burgers and chips!"

"It's pronounced keen-wah, darling… and don't be so smart," her mum would say. The case was always closed when it came to food and nutrition. Her mother had several degrees, diplomas or whatever on that subject and would always win. *If only you knew, Mother dear, that I stuff my face every break-time with sugar*, thought Rachel.

Once, Rachel had spotted a Mars Bar in the fridge and shook it at her mum, accusingly.

"Yes, dear, it's for you," her mum had said. Rachel had given her an odd look then started to unwrap it to shove it into her mouth. Her mum had stopped her.

"No! You can cut it into seven equal pieces and have one bit a day."

The more her mum tried to control what she ate, the more she wanted junk. There were enough people at school who gave her money to address her daily sugar fix.

Rachel knew the dreaded day would come when people would start to notice her hair and she hated the world that it was Jonathan who'd been the first one. That was also the day she'd started to wear a hat, as much as she could get away with, to hide the widening patch on her crown, until one evening at dinner, after being asked to remove it several times, her mum had finally shrieked so loud that everyone in the street must have heard.

"*We are not common Rachel Shill! Now take off that hat at the table this instant!*"

Her dad had looked long and hard at Rachel as she'd slipped the velvety purple hat off and sat there, with strands of long black hair in her hands, eyes wide and staring straight at her mum who stood up aghast, and went promptly to the bathroom to throw up her chicken casserole. She couldn't bear anything to be out of place. Towels had to be facing the right way. The toilet must be cleaned after each use. Books on the shelf were in alphabetical order and the rugs on the floor, perfectly straight and aligned with the wall. Everything in life had to be just so. And now her own daughter was out of place.

And there was nothing she could do to fix her.

Rachel opened the window wider in her room as fat, wet tears ran in zig-zagged lines down her face and the rain, now in tune with her wishes, started to really bang down hard on the earth, beating it into submission like a warlord's drum, ready for battle. She felt a sense of calm wash over her as the rain fought harder to penetrate the gardens, the wind ripping a few flower heads from their stalks and forcing them to journey on a stream down to the drains. She held her hands up out of the window, lifted her face and her hairless head to the sky and screamed with the rain.

"I want to be away from all of this! Why doesn't anyone understand? Why doesn't Moira contact me anymore? Why don't I have a single person in my life who loves and understands me?"

Rachel felt as if her tightly wound up heart was unraveling, spiralling and uncoiling to stretching point, pulling her through space and time, wanting, waiting, feeling inferior to the entire world around her. She started to laugh and imagined what a spectre her mother must think her now if she could see her, like one of those ugly wicked witches from a Roald Dahl novel, their heads all itchy and covered in sores.

"I hate you!" she shouted.

She fell to the floor, wet from the rain and felt strong, loving arms scoop her up and carry her downstairs. Her dad put her in his office on the sofa, covered her with a blanket and held her shaking hands as she fell into a deep sleep.

CHAPTER 15

JOHN

"Miss Timms, you can send Mrs Wrenton into my office now."

John Roody tapped his ballpoint-pen impatiently on the desk, his room full of the aroma of coffee, a new freeze-dried instant kind that he favoured, and some tall wavering lilies which made his nostrils feel like they were burning from the inside out. There was a tiny iced chocolate cake on his desk and a candle that had been lit and then snuffed out. The smoke still lingered. He pressed the intercom buzzer that connected him to Janice Timms next door.

"And I think the lilies need another home Miss Timms… like in the bin please! They are *stinking* the place up!"

He didn't know how the lilies had got there in the first place, but he suspected they were from his secretary, whose own office was always full of plants and flowers, her window wide open even in winter. John only had one thing on his mind at the moment and it was making him feel such a range of emotions he wasn't sure if he could last the term. "Certainly, Sir! Mrs Wrenton, you may go in now," Janice instructed the weary form teacher who'd been waiting outside for at least the past hour.

John could hear his staff talking outside.

"You know what Janice, why not just call me Shirley. Like everyone else does here. OK?" Shirley Wrenton said. He could see her through his door which was slightly ajar, trying to look dignified and also pretty wretched and tired. She was probably annoyed that she'd been made to wait for so long and by the look of the folder she was holding, also probably thought that the reason he wanted her in his office was to talk about end of year testing and reports.

Janice frowned at Shirley and then pinged a polished golden bell. She nodded her head towards John's door, then busied herself with filing.

John stood up awkwardly as Shirley came in, his hair ruffled and tie slightly askew. He glanced at her and she gave him an odd look, as if she was trying to figure out what was going through his mind. He narrowed his glare, not meaning to pull a face, it was just that his eyes ached so much. She probably thought he hated her.

"What seems to be the problem, John?" Shirley asked, sounding impatient and not thrilled at all to be there. "I've got a hundred essays to mark by the end of the day. Is it about the tests?"

She eyed the cake and candle suspiciously. He was sure she noticed the bags under his eyes.

John rocked his chair side-to-side for a few moments and then lifted up the photo frame on his desk. Shirley tried to get a glance but he turned it towards himself. He put his finger on it and traced the outline of the people on there.

"So, Mrs Wrenton...I..."

"Please... John! Call me Shirley. I've felt... *official* all day long and I think by now we can call each other by our first names, don't you?"

John looked extremely uncomfortable and moved his tie around whilst trying to flatten his hair. *She must think I am an idiot,* he thought.

"I've been thinking... and I, um... wanted to run it past you... well, I..." John started to feel a hot red flush spring to his cheeks. Shirley, looking intrigued, sat down opposite him and laid her hands out, hoping he would somehow mirror her openness. He laughed as he knew all his staff had learned this trick in positive behaviour management training and it seemed to work well with the children. Shirley kept her hands open and John took a deep breath. Did laughing make him look crazy?

"Mrs… Shirley… I wanted to thank you for, er, helping me to deal with the Melanie Stoakes case."

"John… this is a school, not a detention centre," Shirley said, reddening slightly, looking even more annoyed. John nodded.

"I've been thinking about her a lot recently you see and well, I guess, I wondered how she was getting on at work experience. She reminds me a lot of someone… and well…"

John checked his blazer pockets, patting himself down slightly manically and then looked up sheepishly as Shirley handed him a tissue from a box that claimed they were for 'men only'.

He mopped his brow and unloosened his tie, his face now glowing like a furnace so much so that Shirley jumped up, slightly alarmed and opened his window.

"John!" she insisted. "Are you… OK? You really don't look OK? Do you want me to call someone? What's going on?"

John hadn't opened up to anyone since Denise in the earlier days of their marriage and he looked at Shirley with her massive earrings and powdered nose. He'd never noticed her properly before. And what a kindly face she had. He hadn't really noticed anything. He coughed, drank a few noisy gulps of water and tried again.

"Well, you see, Shirley… I have a daughter you know.

She's about the same age as Melanie Stoakes. I… I think I've been a bit hard on the girl. I've been thinking about it a lot and, well, just wondered if you could let me know how Melanie is doing. It's… it's my daughter's birthday today. I always… well, I always buy a little cake and light a candle, you know, just to mark it in some way. It's been a while since I spent her birthday with her."

Shirley looked as if she was carefully considering her response. Janice popped her head round the door, asking if they wanted tea and they both looked up at the same time and she caught on quickly, retreating backwards from the room as if bowing to a king in his castle.

John put his head in his hands, his voice quiet and muffled against his blazer sleeve. "You see, Shirley… I don't think I'm very well at the moment. I might have to… take leave for a while. I haven't seen my daughter…" he stopped, realising he was repeating himself and his voice choked. He felt like he was betraying himself and he could hear his mother's voice telling him to *be strong*. He fought the overwhelming urge to burst into tears as he did once, only once, as a child in front of his father who promptly told him to stop.

Young men don't cry.

Keep your chin up and put your best foot forward.

John put the photo frame into Shirley's hands. It was a beautiful black and white photo of a young girl and a much older man. They were looking at each other and the girl had a sweet smile that seemed to curve deeper on one side of her mouth and a dimple on her left cheek. They were holding hands and sitting on a fallen tree stump in what looked like a forest clearing.

"This is my father... and this is... well, this is Bethan. My daughter. I don't see her any more and well, I don't see him either. I pay for his residential fees and honestly, that's about the only input I have in his life. He... he wasn't always the best father but he was a jolly good grandfather."

"Wow!" breathed Shirley. "John... this is really wonderful. Thank you for sharing this with me... that must be hard not to see your little girl?"

"Well, as I said... she must be around Melanie Stoakes' age now. Every time I see Miss Stoakes... Melanie... all I see is Bethan. I get letters from time-to-time but, well, that's really it at the moment...and not even that..."

Was he saying too much? Why was he telling Shirley all this information anyway?

John felt his heart start to implode in his chest, like ripples, waves, currents swooshing out, a new sensation he'd never experienced before, except perhaps when he'd fallen in love with Denise all those years ago. Except this didn't feel good in any way. *There was a time when they had loved each other, right?*

Shirley kept her hands open on the table. They shook slightly. John looked at her thinking, *You're right Shirley... you are the only one that knows. Maybe this is the reason you're here, in Chiltern High, at this moment, just to hear my sad, sad story.*

"My dad... well, George, he's at the home not too far from our school. I got a call recently to say he's taken a bit of a turn for the worse... and I never went to see him." John couldn't stop the tears now. Shirley looked like she didn't know whether to stay or go. She got up from her side of the table and joined him, handing him a huge wad of the oversized tissues, emptying the box, and he swiped at his face quickly, horrified that anyone was witnessing this moment.

"John, I am so, so sorry! I never realised everything you were going through. You know, we would do well to have more staff talking together like this. It's good for us you know... no matter what we may have been told in the past, or..."

John interrupted, sounding like he was being half-strangled.

"Sunny Well... that's the name of the home! That's where he's been all these years and I haven't been to see him, not once! He must think I blame him for what happened... but I don't! I really don't!" John was practically wailing now much to his own alarm.

He put his head down on the table and wept, a flood of lost years, pain and emotion leaking out. He felt like his heart was full of oil, rotten wood and slimy creatures that lived deep within the earth. What had he become? No wonder his own child didn't want to see him anymore. He hated himself for being so weak, so broken. He cried silently, his body shaking and heaving.

"*Please*... please leave!" he said, his voice raspy and gritty.

Shirley half-got out of her seat and wavered. "*Get out!*" John said, not looking up, not making eye-contact. Shirley slipped out of his office and he could hear her saying to Janice in what she probably thought was a low voice,

"It's best we leave him now. Please make sure no-one disturbs him for the rest of the day."

"Is it about the end of year tests?" Janice said, looking over at John.

"Yes, yes it is," Shirley replied quietly and she left the office, her feet making quick steps on the polished floor.

CHAPTER 16
GEORGE

George lay on his bed, slippers still on his feet as he'd been too preoccupied to take them off. He felt like he was skipping on air. He knew it was Bitsy as soon as he'd seen the colour of her hair. She'd grown up, that was for sure! He went to turn the kitten around in his hands and felt confused for a moment as to why it wasn't there. He felt like something was missing but he wasn't sure what. A flash came into his mind of screeching brakes, and a loud scream that could have been an adult female.

His heart beat faster and then, came the knock on the door.

He could hear Sally's voice.

"George, can we come in? Someone would like to meet you... properly!"

He heard hushed tones outside and he felt worried. Were they talking about him as usual? He knew he shouldn't miss this chance. He heaved himself off the bed and padded to the door. Sally came in with the girl. Her hair was tied up in a pony tail, her cheeks flushed bright crimson and she held the ceramic kitten in her hand. He frowned slightly. "Hello… George," said Melanie and offered him the kitten back. "I… I think this belongs to you?" George took the kitten, delighted to see it again and a little confused as to why it had left his hands and started turning it round and round as he always did.

Sally nodded at Melanie then said brightly, "I'll just be down the hall, pet, checking up on Rachel. I've got another load to give her to fold! Have fun! If you need me, just call."

George wished he had a cup of tea or something to offer his Bitsy. It was years since they'd seen each other and she seemed a little… well, lovely as usual but distant?

"How have you been, dear?" George asked, his voice small and fragile as he tried to recall his memory of the bike.

"George, I have come to help for two weeks with work experience…" Melanie said, wanting to add that she was not Bitsy but remembered Sally's fervently whispered words.

"Melanie, listen! Something amazing has happened. I haven't seen George this happy in… well, forever! If he thinks you're Bitsy, then firstly, she must be someone very special to him and secondly, if you don't mind and it doesn't make you too uncomfortable, maybe just go along with it?"

"OK... but what if it makes him more upset if he finds out I am just a girl from the local school on a work placement?" asked Melanie.

"Let's just try. You know... his memory isn't great and he seems to have instantly attached to you. I've read articles about this. It can cause even more distress if we don't go along with it. Lord knows I've spent many a time chatting with dear George about his adventures sailing to China! Give it a try pet, OK?" implored Sally. "If anyone asks, I'll say it's my fault."

George's room was quite small and he knew he should leave the door open when he had visitors. He dragged the chair up next to his bed and motioned for Melanie to sit down. She did so and looked around. Beige and grey paint on the walls, brown and yellow striped curtains and a paisley pattern in green and gold on the bedspread. It was not easy on the eye.

"I guess you're at school now, eh dear?" said George, looking carefully at Melanie. "How old are you now then?"

"Fifteen..." Melanie replied. "And a few months!"

There was a silence as George's eyes glazed over. He could hear the shouting again, the high pitched scream.

"Do you... do you still cycle, love?" he asked, tentatively.

"Not so much really...I guess I didn't really ever take to riding a bike."

George felt a memory pushing to the surface and he tried with all his might to grab onto it, like a fleeting dream before it buried and wove itself into the depths of his mind again. He spoke quietly, almost as if not to disturb a sleeping baby.

"Our breath heated the air and the frost on the grassy verges crunched and crinkled underfoot. As if we were caught in the middle of a real live fairy tale, the moon was suspended directly in the middle of the path, in between the two lines of trees. It was a giant eye, watching over us in its awe and majesty..."

"How beautiful!" Melanie said, frowning slightly. George looked startled. He didn't realise he'd spoken out loud but he continued anyway. He put his hand out in front of him as if trying to reach the reverie his mind seemed to be creating.

"We stood waiting, ears alert, expectant... we didn't know what for. Everywhere appeared to be deathly silent. But I wasn't scared. Ellie looked down at me, affection-ately, as she could see my ears were positively eager to hear some sort of forest activity. '*George, darling... beneath the silence, the air is never quiet.*'"

George put his hand up to his ear and felt the warmth as if it was yesterday.

"I scarcely dared to breathe as she said those words,

as delicately as a spider weaves its web. I held my breath, closed my eyes and all of a sudden... the forest seemed to come alive with sounds I had not heard before. I could hear the murmur of a brook, which rippled so far away... but now the sound was as clear as a bell! I became calmer and then I could miraculously hear the scuffling of tiny feet. A mouse? A shrew? Who knew! It didn't matter. The air became animated with sound and colour and finally I felt I could breathe it all in, savour the feeling of merely existing and being blessed with all my senses. My breath became one of the distinct sounds, all of which appeared increasingly dynamic the less I tried to hear them.

"Ellie, my beautiful wife... we spent so many wonderful times together before... before she passed on. She taught me how to listen, how to love. I really loved her, dear... I really did. And I loved my son... but I never truly showed it. I didn't know how, until... until it was all too late!"

George's eyes started to water a little and Melanie looked hurriedly round the room and finally found a box of tissues, awkwardly handing him one.

"Er...tell me more about... Ellie. I bet you loved her very much," said Melanie, wondering if she was saying the right thing.

George looked wistfully beyond the room, hearing the

sound of waves crashing... always waves. His mind was full and empty at the same time. Why was he here? Who was this person sitting next to him? He looked carefully at the girl in his room. He knew in that precise moment that she wasn't really his granddaughter. His Bitsy would have thrown her arms around him, called him Gramps and would have recognised the kitten. He shook his head and held his hand out to Melanie.

"OK, love... I'll tell you more about my wife Ellie. She was the most beautiful thing I'd even seen. And when our son was born, John, his name was..." George faltered as if trying to get the facts straight. "John was a difficult baby and he would have these awful temper tantrums. Honestly, I didn't know how to block that awful sound out. His legs... they weren't right. I felt... embarrassed by him at first. Luckily I was working away most of the time but when I came back, I saw Ellie with her beautiful smile and hair that glimmered in the sun... and she'd ask me to hold John and I always made some excuse. Perhaps... perhaps that is why when... when Bitsy was born, everything changed. My son put her straight into my arms. That didn't happen in our day you know. The men folk were separated from their wives when they had *our* babies and we never really got to bond... so, so sad when I think about it now."

Melanie listened, her eyes fixed on George. George wiped a few more tears away and continued.

"Bitsy… she was the girl that perhaps I had always wanted. She held onto my finger like a little spider monkey. It all just went horribly wrong one day. Her mother, her awful mother…"

George suddenly felt his heart turn sour as he thought about John's wife.

"She didn't like me and Bitsy being together. She didn't seem to like John or actually, come to think of it, anyone at all. Now, how could you not find a space in your heart to love my Ellie, eh?"

Melanie nodded, wondering how long she'd be expected to sit and listen but also strangely enjoying the interaction. She noticed that he was referring to Bitsy as a separate person now. Did he no longer think she was his granddaughter? She wished she could meet her.

"No, she didn't like anything or anyone. I don't know why… she had a bitter heart that one. I can't remember her name…"

"George… shall I see if I can get you a cup of tea?" Melanie asked.

George narrowed his eyes.

"How many sugars do I take in my tea, Bitsy?" he asked.

They both looked at each for what seemed like the

longest moment and started to laugh. George rolled his head back and his little paunch belly wobbled whilst his shoulders heaved up and down. Melanie couldn't resist and joined in until they were both hitting their own legs, their chests aching.

"I think I might have a heart attack, although I shouldn't joke about that at my age. So dear… what is your name and tell me a little about yourself?"

Melanie blew her nose and realised that her laughter had turned to tears.

"I'm Melanie Stoakes," she said. "And I miss my dad so much. I… I just don't know when he is coming back. He didn't say. He just left one day! One night, he was playing me records and then in the morning, he'd just gone. I knew all the warning signs were there… they'd been there my whole life. But I thought that was normal. That was normal for our family. Anyway! He'd sit for hours on his chair. I'd come in and say goodnight to him and he'd just sit there, staring out of the window. I knew he loved me but… even I couldn't get through to him."

Melanie was sobbing now and her tissue was falling apart.

George made soft clucking noises just like he used to for Bitsy when she was upset as a baby. "And the worst thing of all… I keep thinking that I am just like him,

George! I go into these long moods and I can't get out of them. Sometimes I am in my room for hours, just staring in the mirror, focusing on all the bad that is happening in my life."

"Carry on dear," said George in the kindest tone he could muster. "Carry on... this is good for you, you know, eh? Get it all off your chest, love!"

"And... there was this one time..." Melanie sat up, her eyes stinging and her nose running. She swiped at her face with her sleeve, beyond caring, feeling like a little girl again. "I heard him and mum talking and... and he was saying about how he couldn't let go of how things were in the past. It made me realise, I don't know anything about his childhood. I don't know what happened to him. I always thought he would be the strong one in my life but really, it's my mum. She's kept us all together and she's loved him through all of this. I just want to know when he's coming back..."

Melanie breathed deeply and felt strangely better, like a thousand weights had been lifted off her shoulders. George looked at her and gave her a lop-sided smile. He handed her back the ceramic kitten and said,

"Maybe, just maybe, your dad is also the strong one. It's not easy to say when things aren't right. Yes, your dad is strong. He knew when to get help. Right?"

CHAPTER 17

MELANIE

Dear Diary,

Today has been the strangest and most amazing day of my life. I can't even begin to explain. Well, first of all, I DID meet Tim at the Rec. It WAS him! He looks nothing like I thought he would... only ever seen him from a distance. Closer up he was... well, he still looks incredible but really, just more normal? Not his eyes though! I noticed his eyes straight away. Deep brown! Where do I even start?

I met Old George. Well, George. He is so lovely and sweet and sad and I don't know why but he reminds me of Dad. It was like something clicked almost straight away, which has never happened before in my entire life. I blubbered like a baby! But I felt like I could say anything to him which was... weird but not weird! Am I making ANY sense?! Sally asked me to visit him in his room whilst Rachel continued folding (hahah! Sorry Rachel!) and it was very special indeed.

Back to Tim! I thought I would feel uncomfortable around him but it all felt so familiar, like we'd been mates for ages. How do I even explain that? Me, Pel Mel Stoakes with a proper friend! Two new friends! I didn't think I'd be chatting away to an old man like George! Me and Tim talked about everything. I even talked about Dad. DAD!!!! I love him so much. Dad, I mean. Maybe one day I will let him read my diary. Tim that is... NEVER Dad!

So dear, dear, dear, dear Diary... has my life has changed? Overnight?! OK, somethings remain the same. Although mum has still been singing and dancing around the house like a proper weird one! I keep giving her looks but she just does that annoying smile she does and keeps humming.

George gave me a little kitten!! Not a real one of course. It reminds me of when I was younger and Mrs Douglas, our neighbour, used to give me those little ceramic animals. I found out recently that if you have the whole collection, you can get quite a bit of money for them. Guess where they are now though? In some other teenager's room I'm sure as mum only went and put them in the charity shop when Dad left, didn't she! I think I might have made a bit of a fool of myself with George. I just let it all out and I mean everything... snot and all! He was so good to me and just listened. To be honest, I'm not sure if he really got everything I was saying but maybe he did. After all, he hasn't seen his family for so long too, even longer than me. I wonder if he'll ever see his son again? It just all made me think so much of Dad and then this giant flood gate opened and my whole heart and guts came spilling out in his room. Rachel looked at me so oddly when I got in the minibus after work.

Sally's so nice. I really like her. I'm super surprised that I'm enjoying it there at Sunny Well. I'd made up my mind to hate it so it's strange that I actually am looking forward to going back. I don't want it to end. I wonder if I can still work there after the placement? Mum would be so pleased. I wonder how much longer George will be alive for. I think that about myself too. Some days I just want to live forever and travel the whole world. And then sometimes I feel... I guess I feel like Dad. I can't believe I'll be 16 this year.

OK... so me and Tim went walking around the Rec and even into the forest bit at the end. I say forest but you know I mean a collection of trees to make our estate look not as naff. Ha ha! I think he's had some sadness in his life. He spoke about how when he was small he was picked on a lot because his hair was longer than most of the boys and his ears stuck out, so much so that he had to have an operation. And guess what! He said we should go out again. And I want to. And I need to add to my fact file... or actually maybe I should get rid of that evidence! But just for the record... Tim likes... THE CURE! And he'd even heard of Steeleye Span although he did call them hippie tripe, just like Mum does! Maybe they'll get along! I will love them forever though! He also likes a band called Bow House (spelling?) who I've never heard of... they sound good though. Must check them out. Tim said they are depressing as hell but in an uplifting poetic way. What? Wonder if Dad has heard of them.

I can hear mum in the kitchen again, and Saul even sounds happy. Signing off now. Pel Mel forever x

CHAPTER 18
SALLY

Sally checked the timer on the oven and saw as usual, she'd guessed correctly within seconds. She waited for the ding of the bell then took out the flax-seed muffins. There was nothing better on a sunny afternoon than to eat warm muffins with jam. She turned off the radio as it had been playing the classics all day and she was ready for her own thoughts. Horatio was purring around her feet and asking for food, miaowing pitifully. She poured some treats into his bowl and gave him a stroke. *His fur used to be so matted* she thought *and now, it's sleek and smooth, just as it should be.* She laid her Sunday paper out on the table, patting its oversized pages down, poured the tea and sat down by the window of her little flat, sighing. She sighed a lot these days she found.

David had given her the usual ride home on Friday and had shared the somewhat disappointing news that Geoff was to be re-married... again.

"I was silly to think I'd have a chance with him," she said

to Horatio. She could see herself reflected in the window. "Sit up Sal!" she laughed. Her shoulders were becoming increasingly stooped these days. She was not even thirty but she often felt like she could be much older. She wished she'd been alive in the fifties with the wide skirts and the fitted tops, a simpler life and more precision to detail. Now, it was all so excessive and fashion was something terrible on the high street.

She thought about work and smiled as she remembered how happy George had been when he'd met Melanie. She bent down to stroke her cat and shared her thoughts with him.

"What a shame the girls are only here for such a short time. You know Horatio, I'm a bit worried about the other girl, Rachel. She was quite withdrawn at first and came off a bit rude. I knew at once I didn't want her with the residents, not at first anyway. I felt a bit harsh giving her all the folding work…but I'm good like that. I know people."

Sally giggled and put her hand to her mouth as if trying to stop the sound escaping from her lips.

"But Melanie had a bit of a spark and I just knew she'd be better off with them. I thought it would've been the other way around for some reason when I met them. Just goes to show that we should never judge a book by its cover. And Melanie and George really hit it off! Now that was a big surprise. I could hear them laughing… so lovely! Never heard George laugh like that in all his time at Sunny Well."

Sally tucked into the muffins and thought about how her time with David had finally come to an end. Their conversation had been a little different this week. As soon as she had got into his car, he had looked at her in a funny way.

"Say, Sally… you look great this evening! That's not normal is it, for someone to look so good at the end of a shift on a Friday evening?"

David had laughed as his car purred away from Sunny Well. Sally had echoed his laughter but had checked herself surreptitiously in the wing mirror. She'd reapplied her make-up before leaving and her hair always looked good in this new style she'd been trying out as it stayed up all day with hardly a hair coming out of place. *Was the pink too much though?*

"So… what are you doing tonight?" David had asked, looking at her sideways, trying to keep one eye on the road.

"Oh you know, the same. I'm sure I'll watch a programme, well, Horatio and I will!" She'd felt tickled by that. David knew she had a cat but it sounded like she had a boyfriend.

"Well… you know that Wendy's out of town this week

so I'll be knocking about on my own," David had said and Sally had nudged slightly more towards the window and crossed her legs away from him. He'd laughed and continued driving.

"You know Sally, you really are quite pretty. I like your style... a lot," he'd added. "Although... the pink is weird. I am just going to say it right now. You'd look so much better blonde."

"Stop the car!" Sally had said quickly, trying to sound as official as possible. "I'll make my own way back on Fridays after work thank you very much. And please, give my regards to your wife."

David had laughed again as she'd slid awkwardly out of the car, banging the door behind her hard. He'd zoomed away and she had hurried straight up to her flat and cuddled Horatio. "I don't need anyone in my life right now. Not like that. *Especially* not like that. You'll do, Horatio my love. Time to come up?"

Sally shook her head as she remembered how annoyed she'd felt at the time. As if he understood, Horatio started purring around her legs and rubbing his head on her shins. She patted her lap and Horatio eagerly leapt up as he always did, alternating paw massages on her thighs and then finally settling down and closing his eyes. "What more could a woman possibly need?" said Sally. "Maybe not everyone has to meet a special person! I'm perfectly content right here, right now, with you, my cuppa and my paper. Do you know what, Horatio? I remember the day I left home and Mum and Dad were standing in the doorway looking so terribly sad! I've had a simple life... nothing major ever happened and I liked it that way... and still do! I remember exploring castles and forests though as a child and I was even taken to stay overnight in a lighthouse once! Ah, my parents! I do love them to bits! Mum always making sure dinner was on the table and Dad just getting on with things. I can't complain. I do wonder sometimes if I should sign up for a charity sky-dive or something!"

Sally smiled and carried on reading the news, checking herself in the reflection one more time.

"Sit up Sal!" she said again. She was already looking forward to next week's work experience. And she was looking forward to getting the bus from now on every Friday after work.

CHAPTER 19

RACHEL

Rachel woke up and saw her dad looking down at her. She suddenly remembered why she was in his den. How embarrassing! She wanted the ground to swallow her up. She'd never let herself go like that before.

"Dad?" she said. "Sorry… that must have looked awful. I feel… I just don't feel…"

Her dad wasn't always the best at saying the right thing at the right time but he leaned over to the table and brought a locked box to the couch and placed it in her hands.

"Open it," he said.

"But… you always said…"

"Just open it," her dad said softly.

She flicked the lever open with her finger and a ballerina sprang into life, dancing and twirling on one plastic leg in front of a cardboard enchanted forest. The tinkly melody wove memories into her ears. She'd heard this before, she was sure, maybe before she could even form words.

"A music box?!" Rachel exclaimed. "But... why?" she almost laughed. Like things couldn't get any stranger. "I always thought that something mysterious and maybe even illegal would be in here..."

She closed her eyes and listened to the notes of the music, holding her dad's hand.

"Look, there's a secret compartment in here," said her dad, lifting up a velvet pocket and revealing a photo. Rachel stared at it, tears starting to form. "Is that me and you and mum?" she asked.

"It certainly is. Look how happy we are. I keep this in here to remind me, every day, just how much my family mean to me. When the arguments get too much, I come in here and just shut the world away. I sometimes forget that you might need to do that too. And that maybe, just maybe, you need me to be there for you a bit more. Am I right?"

Rachel leant her head on her dad, still holding the photo.

"Mum looks so pretty here, Dad... I heard you bought her a new lawn-mower!"

"And they say romance is dead!" laughed her dad.

"Do you... do you still love her?" asked Rachel. "I hardly ever see you do things together any more. Is this how all marriages end up? If it is, then I don't ever want to get married!"

"Love… marriage isn't always about the garden looking amazing and roses blooming all year round. You have to both put in a lot of work behind the scenes too, just like we plant the bulbs in the autumn and then in the spring we get all those lovely daffodils. I guess that's like us in some way. But you know what? It works. I wouldn't want to be with anyone else."

"OK Dad," said Rachel. "Can I ask you one more question? Can you please get rid of those birds. I mean, set them free? I feel so sorry for them being in here. Every time I see them, I just feel so… trapped! They've got these beautiful wings and they can't even use them. Dad… that's how I feel! I know there's more inside of me than I let on. I know I'm not the horrible person I seem to be! Oh you wouldn't even understand 'cause you don't see me at school! I am so ashamed of things I've done. I can't take back the words I've said to some people. I always feel so powerless."

"Would that really make you feel better?" asked her dad. "Letting the birds go, I mean? And I *knew* you came in here! You always left a little clue behind Rach!"

Rachel smiled, enjoying this time with her dad so much. The mere act of him carrying her and holding her had reminded her of how much she was loved by him. And she needed to feel that love more than ever right at this moment. "You got me," said Rachel. "And… it really would… make me feel better, I mean. To set them free. You know, losing my hair has not been the worst thing in the world when I think about it. Yes, it sucks BIG time! But what I miss most is the feeling of being part of something. Losing my hair has changed everything. But now everyone hates me. It really is all my fault. I don't belong anywhere anymore."

Rachel cried onto her dad's chest, even though she didn't want to and felt her body shaking.

"OK… I've got an idea. Let's do this now," her dad said. He gently prised Rachel from his body and took her hands and placed them on the cage. The two birds were fluttering around, trying to peck at Rachel's fingers through the little bars.

"Open their door and see what happens," said her dad.

Rachel opened the door and the birds stayed in their cage.

"Come on little things… don't you want to be free?" Rachel tried to encourage them to hop out. "Come on! You don't have to be in your cage any more."

"This is what they do," said her dad. "This cage is all they've ever known. They're actually quite happy to stay in there. Or maybe they're just conditioned to tolerating their environment. Maybe one might fly out and have a little explore around the room but they always come back.

But you… you have the whole world at your finger tips Rach… you can open your cage door anytime and fly as high or as far as you want. OK? We all can!"

"OK. I guess… we're not as trapped as we think we are? Sometimes I feel that I'm just trapped in my own cage, my own thoughts about who I am, or who other people think I am. But they don't really know me… not the true me. I know I can do better… I just can't find the words most of the time."

Rachel's dad looked at her lovingly. "But I know you! I know what you've been through and I know that does not define you. You can do anything, go anywhere, be anything you want to be. You have choices about everything. OK, not everything… I know losing your hair has been really, really tough on you and we don't talk about it openly enough. And we should. Your mum… she's found it really hard and I don't want to excuse her behaviour but you have to know it comes from a place of loving you."

"Is that what love looks like?" said Rachel sadly. "That I will never be good enough in her eyes because I'm broken?"

"No love…and you are the strong one. Your mum needs help and I'm trying but maybe it's not enough. I reckon we could do with having some proper family time together, away from it all, go for long walks in the forest and talk about everything."

Rachel wiped her tears and nodded.

"But in the meantime you and me and all of us *can* choose how to react. I choose to stay with your mother and make it work because it makes sense to me. I love her. People don't know her like I do. She's trapped, just like the rest of us. But I reckon in time, things will change. Especially if we talk more about things. That always helps."

Rachel closed the cage and looked at the birds. "I know I'm only behind my own bars as long as I keep creating them for myself. I know what I need to do. I've got a plan, Dad!"

CHAPTER 20
MELANIE

The phone rang and Melanie ran to get it straight away. Picking it up and feeling the weight of the receiver in her hand was a new experience but she was starting to enjoy it.

It made her feel warm inside.

"Hey Mel… are you free? Fancy a walk?" asked Tim. *Funny,* thought Melanie, *how just yesterday, my heart flipped over backwards hearing his name and now it feels like I'm talking to Saul. How could it change in such a short space of time?* She could hear music in the background.

"What's that you're listening to?" she asked. "Debbie Gibson?"

"Funny," Tim replied dryly. "I actually quite like 'Shake Your Love'."

"Er… I'm no longer free!" Melanie said. *Am I really making jokes now* she thought. She laughed and curled the phone cord around her finger. "Sure! I'll be out in twenty minutes. Shall we start at the Rec again?"

"Yep… I will be there. With flowers on my shirt."

Melanie felt like she could burst with happiness. Two days in a row, hanging out with a friend. An actual friend! And her mum had seemed so happy at breakfast, giving Melanie one of those lingering holds where you're not sure whether to break away or not. In the end, Melanie had relaxed into her mother's soft body as she must have done when she was a child. It was Dad who'd hugged her most. This had felt nice though.

"Pel Mel!" her mum called. "I need to talk with you before you go out!"

Melanie raced downstairs and hopped from one foot to another, eager to get out to meet Tim.

"Hurry up, Mum!" she said, annoyed at the delay.

"Hang on, love… I really do need to talk with you. Pel Mel… your Dad…"

Melanie looked at her mum, her breath starting to leave her body quickly as it always did when anxiety hit.

"Breathe Mel… breathe in and out," Angela hurriedly instructed. "Slower! OK, listen my love! Your dad… your dad is coming out of hospital *this* Wednesday. He's coming back home! How do you feel about that?" Angela's eyes sparkled brightly and her whole face seemed to shine.

Melanie felt as if oxygen was being pumped into her lungs. A flash of images passed through her mind as she thought about all the things she might be able to do again with her dad. *Her dad!* She pushed her head into her mum's shoulder and burst into tears.

"I feel good," she spluttered through her sobs. "Really good." She also felt worried. What if Dad didn't look the same? Smell the same? What if he didn't call her his Baby Beet anymore?

"It's going to be OK," soothed Angela. "It might be a bit different but he's really looking forward to seeing us all. He's really ready to come back. We'll take it all slowly, a step at a time. He's already warned me that he has a big hairy beard now! I'll be shaving that off in his sleep before he knows it! Pel Mel… he's on medication and it's really helping him. We'll be fine. We'll do this together."

Melanie looked at herself in the mirror in the hallway and saw the usual pox scars, a couple of angry-looking spots and tear-stained cheeks. *I look a right state now* she thought. *Thanks a lot Mum! Tim won't care anyway. And nor do I.* It felt weird to leave her mum after hearing such big news but Angela had already sprinted upstairs and Melanie could hear the vacuum cleaner whirring and her mum singing Kirsty MacColl at the top of her voice.

Melanie made her way to the Rec and Tim was already there, sitting casually on one of the tyre swings, the chains making the most hideous grating sound. He was wearing a velvet flowery shirt. Melanie laughed.

"Nice! And you were saying what about hippies? How can you deal with that noise?" she said and Tim looked up and smiled.

He is handsome Melanie thought. *An unusual type of handsome. It's a wonder he doesn't have all the girls chasing after him at school.*

Tim shifted off the swing and they started walking together, in silence at first, which felt good. Melanie tried to form words, ready to share. After all this time, how could she say that her life was set to change? Would they stay put or move again? Could her dad work? She had so many questions. She felt like a bottle of soda that had been shaken up but still had the lid on. Tim started to talk at the same time as Melanie and they both laughed. "You first," said Tim. "I was just going to ask if you're OK?"

"My Dad is coming back to live with us on Wednesday!" Melanie blurted. "I know you don't know much about it all but… it's good news! I think it's good news… it IS! I feel like I could tell you anything," added Melanie as they meandered down the road past the silt bins. She hoped she wasn't saying too much or being too forward. It felt natural to say exactly what she was thinking to Tim.

"Yeah, me too… you know when you started at our school, I really wanted to come and talk to you but you seemed… so distant. I think a lot of us thought you wanted to keep yourself to yourself."

Tim fidgeted with a button on his shirt when he said this.

"By the way, that's really great…about your dad I mean. I hope he's better and that it all works out."

"It is… it actually is." Melanie sighed. Tim's calm mood was so relaxing. She put her hand in her pocket to find a tissue and felt the little ceramic kitten from George nestling there. She turned it round in her fingers as she continued.

"You know, I don't always like to hang out with people. I do like having friends of course… well… just not lots of friends. I look at the girls at our school and don't feel I fit in with any single one of them. My mum says I need to stop being so picky and give people more of a chance. But what they talk about is so… boring! Literally, I have no interest in talking about who loves who, what's going on with the latest soap opera… I just feel like there is more to life, you know?" Tim was quiet for some time.

"I get it…" he said. "I have the same thing with the lads. I… I don't really identify with the things they say. They talk a lot of brave talk you know… I just want to get on with my art really."

"You're an artist?" said Melanie. "Can I see something you've done?"

Tim laughed. "I didn't say I was an artist! I just said I want to do it! I love painting. Not the standard type. It's all quite abstract."

They stopped and sat down on the kerb. Melanie picked at the grass that was pushing through the concrete and twisted it round her fingers. She thought about saying she liked to draw birds and swirling doodles but kept quiet. The art of listening to a friend was new and intriguing.

"I try to paint feelings…" Tim continued. "You know, I was in therapy for a while as a kid. I wasn't bonding with the people at school and my parents got me seeing someone about it. But I was just happy, and I mean really happy, to be on my own. I always felt I was the square peg in a round hole… do you know what I mean?"

"Er…exactly!" Melanie said. "I feel like that the whole time! I always feel I need to put myself slightly on the outside. If I get too much *in*, if you know what I mean, then I feel like I'm getting lost. I feel more… I dunno, more *whole* when I'm alone."

Tim gave Melanie a sideways glance and grinned. "Present company excepted?" he ventured.

"Of course!" Melanie replied. "You're… different. I really love hanging out with you and we only just met! I have a little confession. Do you want to hear it?"

"Sure, but then I'll share something too. OK?"

Melanie's heart fluttered in nervous anticipation.

She already hoped now that Tim didn't like her that way. He felt like a long-lost brother. Everything felt so familiar and *safe* with him. She made a mental note to throw her diary entries away. Melanie continued. "OK... you know I just said how much I hate all the girly stuff at school... well, I still had a massive crush on you! I mean... I wrote about you in my diary and everything!"

Tim laughed out loud when she said that and they both got up and carried on walking, weaving across the different streets, noticing big sofas that had been discarded and waiting for the council to pick them up, damp and soggy from the recent rain.

"Melanie... you're really lovely, but... I never liked you in that way. I always thought you looked... a bit different and interesting. I just don't feel like that about anyone at the moment. Maybe I will in the future but... maybe it's because I'm just so focused. I do really love hanging out with you. This is new to me too, you know?"

"Wait... you think I am 'lovely'? Can we just back-track to that bit please!" laughed Melanie. "I don't think anyone has ever said that about me before. Not anyone who's my age anyways."

"Well, you should hear what some of the boys at school say about you," said Tim looking down, scuffing his feet on the pavement. "Trust me Mel, you'd be able to get a boyfriend in a flash if you wanted."

"YUK!" groaned Melanie.

"Yuk?" laughed Tim. "How old are you? Five?"

They both laughed. It felt so good to be with someone you could say anything to.

"Yeah… apart from my crazy crush on you, which by the way NO-ONE knows about, I don't think about people like that at the moment either. I guess… I guess I put a lot of *my* focus on my dad. I think about him a lot, you know. He's always just there, on the back of my mind. Whatever I'm doing, I'm thinking about him, even if not consciously. And when I hear certain songs, my heart just cracks into pieces. Wow… that was probably a bit too deep."

"Do you want to talk about it?" asked Tim. "You can bend my ear anytime you like."

"Bend your ear? How *old* are *you*?" laughed Melanie.

"Ninety? Well, it's weird. I don't talk about him. We don't at home. We just all get on with it. He's mainly always been like that. I guess it's… depression? Sometimes he looks like he's been crying but for a long time. And his eyes… they often look like he's focusing on something far away, thinking about something, playing something over and over. Sometimes he's looking at me but I don't think he sees me. It's like… he's looking past me. I hate it when he does that. I think he's got a diagnosis but he never shared it with me. Him and mum… they're really close. He said he'd talk about it more with me when I'm older. Maybe he wants to protect me? I see so much of myself in him it's scary. But I also know I'm not him. I just can't believe he's coming home! At one point, I really thought I'd never see him again. But you know what, it's weird… even when he's not there, like physically, at home, I just feel he is. Does that sound strange?"

Tim put his hand to his chin and stroked a line of light stubble. "Really strange!"

Melanie hit him on the arm.

"We get on well though, don't get me wrong. I just take it for granted I guess that my dad is like this. Don't forget you were going to tell me something too."

"Another time," said Tim. "Look, we're nearly back at the hill. Let's get you home."

"By the way, where are you for work experience week?" Melanie asked. "Where have you been going whilst I've been having the time of my life at Sunny Well?"

"The pizza factory on the industrial estate," replied Tim.

Melanie laughed and nearly choked on her spit. "You're kidding! Really? That's so rubbish!"

176

"Well," said Tim, "there were no artist studios to go to and I left it late. So the school sorted me out. But... I get as much frozen pizza as I want!" His eyes twinkled.

Melanie felt magnetised towards Tim, like she needed to be in his embrace. As if he read her mind, he opened his arms and beckoned. He was wearing what looked like a handknitted black jumper, even though it was warm out, which was too long and the sleeves hung over his hands. The ends were fraying, as if he'd worn it for a very long time.

They hugged each other. His shoes had holes in and she could see one of his white socks poking through. It felt so good to be in his arms. He reminded her of her dad. Maybe it was the smell? There was something about him. She wanted to stay there for a long time.

"OK, off you go!" Tim said. "Oh and by the way, I forgot to bring a new record with me. I think you might like this band... groundbreaking stuff. Makes chills go down my spine."

"What are they called?" asked Melanie enjoying everything about this moment.

"You'll see. Music will never be the same again for you once you've heard the whole album. And make sure you do... listen to the whole album, OK? On repeat."

"Ha!' said Melanie. "My dad says that, well... *said*

that a lot. But of course! How else does one listen to one's music?"

Melanie laughed as they went their separate ways and felt a big ball of fire in her belly, warm and cosy, the place to toast marshmallows and snuggle down in sleeping bags. A campfire of loveliness.

She went straight into the living room where Saul was playing a game with their mum.

"Mel, guess what! Guess WHAT! Dad's coming back! Dad is coming BACK!"

"I know Saul… isn't that great?"

She put her hand on his shoulder and then went upstairs and held her pen over a fresh page of her diary.

"Looks like I got it all out today, dear Diary," Melanie said to the paper on her desk and put her stereo on instead.

CHAPTER 21

GEORGE

I have a distant thought in my head that I'm in the ocean surf, chasing an object. I'm six years old. Everything is bigger, brighter and better than I usually remember. People line the beaches like they have never seen the sea before. Samuel is there of course. He always is when I focus hard enough. His blue eyes match the sea. He has the sky in his eyes. Every movement occurs in slow motion (as it's supposed to, apparently) and Samuel is the one who is chasing the object. I think it was a ball…

George had been writing all morning and his head felt clearer than it had in a while. He wanted to capture this feeling and keep it going as long as possible. Sally had sheepishly told him this morning that Melanie was coming to visit him again today. He'd nodded at her and patted her arm, which he'd hoped conveyed the right amount of sentiment that everything was just fine and dandy. He didn't quite have the words to talk it through. It was a win-win situation, he'd thought.

There was a knock on his door and he stood up to let his visitor in. It was amazing how much Melanie looked like Bitsy. Well, as much as his memory would allow. He'd formed this idea of exactly how Bitsy should look and then that idea morphed into Melanie. Sally stood behind her and he heard her say quietly,

"Everything OK or do you want me to stay?"

"It's fine," replied Melanie grinning widely at George. "We had a great time last time, didn't we?"

Sally left the door open and ventured down the hallway, feeling a bit like a spare part. She didn't need to do half her jobs now the girls were here.

"Good morning George!" said Melanie. "I think lunch is about to be served so we have a bit of time, you know, if you want to chat."

"Well, of course!" George exclaimed with a feeling that he could only suppose was delight and hurried back to his desk and continued writing. He felt so joyful today. George read out loud as he wrote.

"Like an elastic band, I am catapulted to the scene. It's a windy day. Mother is standing on the shore. Beautiful. Round belly. Blue full body swimming attire. Long, golden hair with hints of auburn, glinting in the sunlight. The fear in her eyes is not recognised by the two playful boys. Their laughter bounces and skims along the crests of the waves and reaches her ears like a sinister calling. A premonition? She has dreamt about this scene. And the story is unfolding before her."

Melanie nodded in appreciation and gave a little clap.

"I'm trying to remember something Melanie, dear," George explained. "And it seems today that I'm having what I like to call *a window of clarity* and I need to use it wisely."

He didn't mention that he'd had griping pains the last couple of days in his stomach and a headache that felt like a whirlwind in his brain. He'd put it down to all the new excitement. He couldn't explain it but he felt something amazing was going to happen, as if he was about to go on a long journey to a far-off land.

"I had a dream about my dear Ellie last night…" he said as Melanie came and crouched down next to him at his desk.

"Tell me more!" Melanie said. "Do you mind if I have a bit of paper? I can draw while you talk. Got a pencil too? Beautiful bit of writing by the way. Did it really happen? Or is it a story?"

George smiled. He loved the easy way Melanie spoke to him.

He fumbled through papers in his desk and found some old scraps and a HB pencil muttering, "That remains to be seen, that remains to be seen. Here… this one is really good for shading. I used to do some fine shading myself when I was a lad. I think I got rid of all my sketches. I see you're wearing the Sunny Well uniform today?"

"Every day, George!" laughed Melanie. "It makes me feel all official. I'm kind of enjoying being here. I didn't want to come here and it's kind of rubbed off on me now. Anything is better than school right now! And I'm so grateful for our chat the other day."

George knew they had talked but some of the details were already beginning to wisp and spire like smoke rising from a fire, dispersing into the sky. He'd managed to hold on to enough to remember the main points by repeating what they had spoken about, muttering the words out loud, hoping that no one would see or hear him, knowing they would think his mind was getting worse. He also knew that Melanie had cried. And that she was not Bitsy. But that strangely, he really loved her being here.

He held his pen over the paper but the words started to edge away, blurring into the lines. He pushed the pen down hard and it marked the paper. He could hear the ocean crashing and the waves washing through his mind, pebbles getting stuck in the synapses of his brain.

"I just can't get this one memory right," he insisted, frustrated. He frowned at the paper as if it was keeping the secrets of his mind from him.

Melanie carried on sketching, two little birds in a cage, trying to add motion with pencil strokes so it looked like the cage was swinging to and fro.

"George, have you tried drawing your memories instead of writing them?" Melanie asked. "Maybe something extra will come if you can make pictures. I always write my diary and then add them in. But I can only seem to draw birds! They mirror how I feel... and the swirls, well, they connect every thing together. I feel like I'm creating a universe when I do this and believe me, I'm not good at drawing!"

Melanie showed him and George whistled.

"Well, those doves look fabulous to me," he said, sounding impressed.

"Hmm... well, they're supposed to be robins, so close enough I guess!" laughed Melanie.

Tracy came in with George's tray of sandwiches, a lukewarm milky tea in a plastic cup with a straw and some biscuits. Both Melanie and George frowned at the tray.

"Well, that looks appetising!" said Melanie, surprised at herself for making a joke.

Tracy winked at her and said, "Just making the rounds! Don't shoot the delivery girl!" and left, pushing a trolley full of meals further down the corridor, the wheels squeaking rhythmically.

"You can tell they're short-staffed when they send her round to bring our meals," said George. "What's her name?"

"Tracy, I think," said Melanie, even though she knew it was.

George took a bite of the sandwich and nodded. "Yes, they have used margarine again. I know the difference between marg and butter you know. Really gets my goat."

Melanie sighed out loud. She felt like she'd been working here for years. Everything felt so comfortable and familiar recently. She wanted to hold onto the feeling as long as she could. Being here really reminded her of being with her dad. She closed her eyes and tried to picture his face. It was fuzzy, like lines were drawn over his features, like a child's scribble. She added a beard to his face in her mind. It was long and almost reached the ground.

"Well, I wonder…" said George. "I keep having an image of a ball, of all things, in my mind. It's one of those lightweight ones that you can float on the water and it keeps slipping out of my grasp. The memory I mean." In his mind, he also saw the ball moving further and further away from him. He frowned as he felt something rise within his belly, working his way up to his chest and then throat. Panic? He already knew that a great sadness had happened in his childhood but it crossed over with his separation from Bitsy. The sound of waves, car brakes and screaming were played like a constant record in his mind. He started to draw a picture of a ball and fumbled around again in his drawer.

"Do you have any colours?" he asked.

Melanie smiled. "Sorry, just the one pencil that you gave me."

"I like you being here," George said. "You certainly don't suffer fools gladly."

"I don't know what that means, but thank you!" said Melanie.

George laughed and it turned into a deep cough. He spat the phlegm into a tissue and tucked it under his pillow.

"Now… I don't know either come to think of it. Suffer fools gladly… that one gets lost on the tongue now." He wrote the word 'red' on the picture of the ball and proceeded to draw two small boys playing in the sea. He showed Melanie.

"Lovely,' she said. "See, drawing helps!"

"Samuel," said George suddenly. "He was my brother.

He kept reaching for the red ball. He had these tumbling yellow locks that always fell in his face. He was a very beautiful young boy… people thought he was a girl. I heard one person, Mrs Cooke if I remember rightly, saying that I was a plain thing next to her. Oh that made me sad! But… I was, plain next to him, that is.

"His face was always sun-kissed with freckles. Our mother had a thing for us being outside. Anything to get away from our dad. We'd always have to be going out, roaming around the streets. This was our first holiday. Do you know what scares me the most, Melanie dear?"

Melanie looked into his eyes and he could almost see himself reflected in hers. *Just like Bitsy,* he thought. He felt a mixture of joy that Melanie was there and regret that she wasn't the one who he wanted to be there the most.

"I…I am scared that one day, I am going to wake up and I won't remember a single thing," he said, his voice suddenly trembling and small. "I will wake up and I will look at myself and not recognise a single part of me. I will read my ramblings in my diary and they won't make sense. And I will be here for years, not knowing, not understanding. And that girl will bring those tasteless sandwiches round and maybe someone will have to feed me them as I will have forgotten how to eat. Do you think it will be like that, dear? Maybe it'll feel like I'm trapped in my mind, like those people in a coma who can hear and see everything but can't move. Did you ever read about those people?"

Melanie reached out and took his hand. It was very soft, a home to decades of wrinkles, purple bruises on his knuckles, a mark where he'd once worn his wedding ring. A scar from a cut many moons ago.

"I didn't read about them George, but I did read about a mum once, who called her baby Elvis! Do you want me to tell you about that?"

George lay on his bed and Melanie sat on the chair, telling him all the headlines she used to read when she delivered newspapers. He drifted off and Melanie wrote a note and put it on his desk.

Dear George,
You fell asleep. We talked about the sea, Samuel and how much you love me coming to visit. My name is Melanie and I am your new friend. I will come and see you tomorrow.

CHAPTER 22

JOHN

John left school early, rushing past Janice who tried to say something about tests and then got into his car as fast as he could, sitting at the wheel, feeling like his head might explode. In the car park there was the usual barrage of pupils gathering around the ice-cream van that turned up after school every day. He questioned himself regularly as to why he'd sanctioned this. It had seemed like such a bad idea at the time.

The people who owned the van were an Italian couple in their fifties and they took turns to come and face the crowds. It was the woman's turn today, trying to serve ice-cream to half-crazed children, who howled like starving wolves, rocking the van back and forth with all their might and chanting something John couldn't figure out. Even from his car, he could see the woman's eyes widen as the van rocked harder and she started shouting at the children to move back and make an orderly line. Taunts of his childhood days echoed in his head and his leg ached. He wanted to go and intervene but couldn't move his body. Those darned kids! The woman didn't look terrified at all but instead managed to hold onto the ice-cream she was serving, the van moving back and forth like a boat in a stormy sea and still take the children's money, like she'd been doing it all her life. *Maybe it's calming*, John thought.

She should put those skills on her CV.

This is what my life has been reduced to. Headteacher of the school, watching my students terrorise the humble ice-cream folk. He couldn't face anyone now.

He probably couldn't face anyone ever again.

John made up his mind right at that moment to take a few weeks off work and then hand his notice in. He was no good at his job. He couldn't protect the pupils, he couldn't protect the ice-cream vendors and he couldn't protect his daughter.

"I am a prize turkey of an *idiot!*" he shouted, banging his hands on the steering wheel and more tears started to run down his nose. He somehow managed to drive home and couldn't get through the front door fast enough.

John threw his leather briefcase on to the sofa in his living room and it bounced a few times then teetered on the edge of the grey throw he'd slung over it to hide the shabbiness. Not that he ever had any visitors anyway. Everything was grey in this house. *It reflects my life*, he thought. He took off his tie then drew the curtains and slid down the wall, onto the floor, trying to control his rasping breath. He'd have to have a check-up. He suspected asthma. And at the rate he was going, a heart-attack some time soon as his blood pressure was so high.

In his hand, he held a letter he'd picked up from the mat a few days ago and had kept in his pocket. He'd recognised the childish scrawl straight away. It had made his heart do a somersault and sick to his stomach. The letters were always too short, never enough information. He always wanted to know more but just got the polite bits. Had he really cried today in front of Shirley Wrenton? His stomach knotted further.

His hands shook slightly as he opened the letter and then the phone rang. It was shrill and pierced through his skull. He held his head and stumbled to answer it. He could have let it ring but he had an idea that it might be Bethan.

"Hello, is that... hello?"

A woman's voice, soft yet official spoke down the receiver. It crackled a bit and he could hear music playing as if on a crossed line.

"Hello, John Roody here," he coughed. He wondered if it was a prank call. He'd had those before. He made a mental note to remove his name from the phone book.

"John, hello... it's Sally Chambers from Sunny Well.

Remember we spoke recently about your Dad, Old…
Mr Roody Senior?"

John remembered the day he had gone to see his
mother just after her operation. His dad didn't know he'd
been and his mother had sworn she wouldn't tell.

"Things are terrible with Denise," he'd complained,
feeling small and lost like he used to. "She's taking Bethan
up to Scotland, to be with her new fellow or whatever
she calls him. I'm sorry, Mum! You know what this means
though don't you?"

His mother had stroked his head and cooed like a dove
at him, then hummed a melody that she had sung to him
when he was a baby.

"Yes, John… it's going to break your dad's heart not
being able to see Bitsy. But she has every right to go. You
can't stop her, love. You can arrange visiting rights through
the courts if you want. Now listen John… I need to tell
you something. And I need to tell you now. Your dad *does*
love you. He has not always been a good dad. I know that
and I know you know that too. I don't want to lie to you
John… but I want you to somehow, one day, make things
up with him and forgive him. He is going to grow old and
be alone. When I go… and I will go soon, he is going to
go downhill fast."

John had held his mother's hand as she told him stories

of when he was a baby and his dad had been out at sea, whilst serving in the Navy.

"One day, I received a notice that your dad's boat had been overturned! It had, but they all survived! Silly things! I thought I was going to be left on my own! I can't be a widow! They're old and grey and have walking canes! Funny how your Dad had terrible sea legs though! You know, his father treated him something rotten. Used to beat him all the way around town. He tried his best with you, son. Try and see that. There was always food on the table and he made sure all your medical treatments were paid for and extra tuition to keep you up to standard at school. I know, I know... he wasn't good with dishing out the love when it came to you. But you got enough of that from me."

His mum had hugged him tight and that was the last time he ever saw her.

"So... John?" Sally asked, hesitant. "Are you still there?"

John coughed again, letting his memories disappear and replied, "Yes, yes, I am here."

"Did you hear what I said? The phone's a bit off today. The sooner you can come, the better, I think. We've noticed some changes from the doctor's report and... well, a lot of them have these moments of clarity before... you know, before..."

"Thank you Miss Chambers. I will be sure to come visit soon," John said. "I promise."

"Just one more thing Mr Roody… I know that something terrible must had happened, perhaps with your… your daughter. Was there an accident or something? It's just that I heard George talking to one of our staff volunteers and… well, I wonder if it's anything we can help with…or you can?"

John went silent for a few moments. He knew what Sally was talking about. His poor Dad!

"Thank you Sally… and… you can call me John".

He sighed as he put down the receiver, trying to push as much breath out from his body as possible. It felt so stale.

He opened the letter from his daughter, Bethan.

Hi Dad,

It's been a while I know. How are you? How is school and being in charge? My hamster died. She (we found out it was a girl) had something called 'wet tail'. Mum said that was enough of pets now.

I wanted to come the last holiday but Mum had something planned with Des. Des and Denise! Honestly Dad… I don't like him. His two sons are annoying and whiny and get everything they want. I wondered how Gramps was doing. I suddenly started to miss him terribly. It's been so long since I saw him last. Mum says he's in a home now and is forgetting things and that he probably doesn't remember me. I don't want him to forget me, Dad. Can I come and see him with you? I also wondered, if it was OK with you… could I come and stay with you for a while? Maybe the next holiday? Mum doesn't know I'm asking. She'll say no I think but if you arranged it with her, maybe that would work?

I got a B plus for my English story the other day. I wrote about the time Gramps nearly ran me over with his car and flattened my little pink bike! I remember mum screaming at the top of her lungs and the sound of the frame of the bike crunching under his wheels. I called it 'Lucky Escape but not for Florence!' Do you remember that's what I used to call my bike? Florence!! My teacher loved it but Mum was mad at me for writing it. I had no dinner that night. I mentioned how loud she'd screamed in my story. I know it happened ages ago but I remember. Well, I got my B plus anyway and I was 'pleased as punch' with that. (We learned that at school recently and I need to put it in a sentence somewhere!) I've enclosed a copy of the story for you to read. My teacher, Miss Baines is really kind. I can understand her better than the other teachers. My accent is starting to change. All the teachers are nice here. Except the art teacher. I don't think she likes me because I 'can't draw for toffee'. Yes! I got another one in. I think they're called idiots or something! Joking! I know it's idioms.

I hope I can come soon. Thanks for my birthday money by the way. Mum said you'd put some into her bank for me. I opened up my own bank account recently so I should give you the details. Oh that sounds cheeky! I wanted to buy some new clothes with my money but Mum said it's going towards the child maintenance that she never gets from you. I had my eye on a really nice outfit too so I am really sad about that.

I miss you Dad. I hope things are ok. Please let me know when I can come and see Gramps and you. I think about him so much right now...I really don't want him to forget me.

Sorry I haven't kept in touch much. Maybe I will more now as I am FIFTEEEN!!!! I've grown up a little bit. I definitely feel much wiser!

Bye Dad, your Bethan

John let the letter slide down onto the floor. He dialled the phone number to his lawyer friend, who picked up straight away.

"Hello, Ted… it's been a long time but I need to get straight to the point. What rights do I have as a father? I want full custody of Bethan."

CHAPTER 23

RACHEL

It was Sunday and Rachel felt like her body was made of lead. Her alarm hadn't gone off and she'd been flitting in and out of dreams for most of the morning. She'd already missed her elocution lesson. She wondered why her mum hadn't barged in as she usually did, checking that she was up at exactly 7:30am, waving a pungent green smoothie under her nose along with a tray of vitamins and potions. She didn't care anymore. She reached for the pink clock with fluorescent hands and gave it a sharp knock. The alarm sprang into effect, a strange and distorted sound escaping from the mini speaker, like a chicken being slowly strangled. Half-amused, and half-feeling sorry for the chicken, she drifted into a somewhat uneasy sleep where dreams assailed her from every side. She swam with giant turtles, flew in between the clouds and rode on a merry-go-round, holding onto someone who sat in front of her. The person turned round and it was Tracy, who spoke and sounded like Jonathan.

I hate you.

She awoke again to the sound of their enormous new lawn mower gnashing at the weeds outside in their garden. Her mum had tried to get her dad to buy of those sit-on models to cover the huge grass area, which was practically a mini-field but they'd gone for the new electric one that still needed to be heaved forward by your entire body weight, despite the motor. She was so embarrassed by it and hoped that the neighbours hadn't noticed. Who was she kidding! The whole street could not have missed that racket.

Rachel dragged each leg out of bed. *Having emotional outbursts was like running a marathon*, she thought. Not that she'd ever run a proper one, just Miss Garner's hideous charity 'mini-thons' as she called them, shouting for the girls to pick their legs up and get moving as they tried desperately to pull their terribly unflattering gym knickers as far down their legs as they'd go.

She managed to get to the window in time to see her mum mopping her brow, sweating profusely. *Glowing* her mum called it. Her dad was pointing to patches of grass her mum had missed, who looked perplexed as the lead twisted around the washing line and trailed over her feet. Rachel swore loudly then switched on the radio which was permanently tuned to Rock FM.

She didn't know the names of most of the bands. She

longed to get her hands on a bass guitar. She always felt the pulse of the bass-line, bringing the song together, making her feel whole, throbbing like a heart beat, pounding into her skull, taking her out of her own body, leaving her clothes, her torso, her hairless head far behind, like it all meant nothing, soaring up into the clouds and feeling like she was hanging out with angels. Her mum of course had said *no* to bass guitar. But *yes* to cello and violin.

Go figure.

The music did something to her body. It was so freeing. She tuned the presenter out as hearing spoken voices on the radio felt like she was grating her nails on a chalk board. She had a seed of an idea and no amount of music was stopping it from growing. She wasn't one for writing but she really needed to speak to Auntie Joan. Phoning her was out of the question. She had a plan. She hoped Joan would be on board. She kicked the bin under the desk and several attempts of a letter from the night before spilled out around her feet, her words screaming up at her.

I don't want to live here anymore. I hate my life here. I want to be away from it all. All I can think about is leaving. Please come and get me.

So juvenile she thought. *I sound like a child having an epic tantrum.*

She took a deep breath and stared at the wig on its stand. She'd been leaving it off on the weekends more now, standing at her bedroom window, feeling the breeze caress her head. She felt for stubble but as usual there was none. Not even a stray hair.

Dear Joan

Too official.

Dear Aunt Joan

No, that made her sound like an old aunt and she was younger than that.

Hello Joan, it's Rachel. I don't know how long this will take to reach you but I wanted to say thank you for all the help you've given me since...

She tried to write, 'Since I lost my hair' in a variety of ways and it all sounded contrived.

"But I *have* lost my hair," she said out loud. "I don't have hair anymore."

She started laughing.

"I am bald, shiny and egg-like. I am like an old man, a

creature from the sea. Maybe I should grow scales. Water slips off me effortlessly in the shower now…"

The words of the song on the radio seared into her brain and Rachel imagined herself at one of the summer festivals she'd heard about, moving her head back and forth to the music, the crowd going wild. What would it feel like to swing her head around with no hair? She tried writing again.

Hello Joan,

I really miss you at the moment. Mum told me about the school you're working in. I'm actually doing work experience at the moment in an old folks' home. It's OK and a bit boring. I don't get to see the residents much as I have to spend most of my time folding bed-linen. I bet you are laughing! Actually, it's been helpful. It's so boring that I'm forced to hear my own thoughts and figure things out a bit.

I am currently in my room listening to music (rock as always – thanks AJ for introducing me) and my window is open. I love it when the wind comes in here. I've been washing my wig like you taught me. That was a really fun day when we went into London. I would love to do that again someday. Are you coming again soon?

I can imagine if you were here now, you'd not be so proud of me.

I haven't been the best version of myself. I feel an anger within me a lot of the time. It bubbles and burns so much that I feel like I'm a nasty soup in a cauldron. A witch's potion, poisonous, ungrateful for life, hateful, full of myself. I don't know what happened. Mum is being impossible. I don't want to talk about her to you, I know you're sisters but I can't stand how she's being. I really want to leave and come and be with you. Could I come and work at your school in Timbuktu or wherever it is that you are! I leave school soon anyway and was going to go to beauty college but now... I just need to get away. I did think about training to make wigs for other girls like me... don't laugh, I'm not joking! Well, it crossed my mind anyway.

There's a girl called Melanie that I work with. Well, I hardly see her at work. I see her looking happy and it makes my heart sink like a stone. Am I really that awful? Why do I want everyone else to be unhappy? I need help Auntie! I need you to come and rescue me.

Rachel threw the letter into the bin and put her headphones on. She didn't know her auntie's address anyway. Words fell into her ears, as the next song blared and the singer crooned his chorus.

She tried to drown out her thoughts but they won,

the music lost. Things kept picking at her, invading her mind. Joan had told her once to Tai Qi her thoughts away, elbowing them into another time and space but she hadn't even come close to being able to do that.

She felt annoyed at the thought of her parents getting on. *Pick and choose when you're in love,* she thought. When had they changed? Was it all her fault that they'd started to argue so much? It certainly seemed so as she heard her name mentioned so many times behind closed doors. Half the time now, her mum didn't ever bother to lower her voice. Rachel closed her eyes and pushed her feet into the warm carpet under her desk as the light from the sun moved further into her room. *I've just crushed a trillion dust mites* she thought.

She looked back out of the window and her parents had disappeared from the garden so she got back into bed, pulling the covers up, even though it was way too hot, feeling the pressure of the duvet pushing down on her like she was being enveloped, a babe in the womb, restricted in her movement, comforting. She could hear voices in the kitchen and wondered if her parents were talking about her. Was her dad letting her mum know he'd found their one and only daughter screaming with all her might to the elements? He hadn't mentioned it since. Not that she'd seen him. Was it their little secret? Did he tell her mum that he'd carried Rachel all the way downstairs, not even flinching, his arms strong and unwavering? She remembered waking up on his couch and he'd been there, on the floor, curled up right next to her. They'd talked more than they had in a very long time. Rachel felt herself smile and a sudden surge of adrenaline rushed through her body.

"Right, enough!" Rachel said out loud. "Times change and so do people. Let's do this!"

Rachel retrieved the crumpled letter from the bin, flattened it out and folded it into an envelope. "Let's hope your address is the one I still have in my book. Auntie Joan!" she said.

CHAPTER 24
MELANIE

"You go first," said Melanie, leaning on the wall, picking off the patterned paper and trying to fold it between her finger and thumb.

"No, you," said Tim. "I like hearing you talk. It's… calming."

"What are you doing right now?" asked Melanie, hearing scraping sounds down the phone.

Tim laughed. "Painting," he said. "With one hand."

"Me too," said Melanie. "Well, not painting. You know what I mean! I like hearing you talk."

She heard the click of the phone which meant her mum had hung up and stopped listening.

"OK, now we can talk properly!" she said and picked a whole patch of paper off, wall crumbling onto the landing.

"Does your mum always listen in on your phone calls?" asked Tim. The scraping sounds continued.

"Well, this is only my third one so, yes! Every single one!" They both went quiet for a moment.

"I was thinking recently about my dad," said Melanie. She lowered her voice a little and could hear her mum talking to Saul.

"When I was younger, I guess I was six, we lived on a different estate. It could have been this one it was so similar. There were always empty milk bottles outside each house. Some of the kids would go round nicking them and filling them with water, you know, like, to play them, making little tunes... I remember this couple who lived nearer the bottom near the pub. They had this lovely window box and they'd painted their fence green. Some people used to talk about them and say they were too posh, doing things differently. I always loved their garden though. It even had a collection of gnomes! Ha! They didn't last long. They kept having to replace them. They were good friends with my dad and they'd be down the pub together a lot of the time on the weekend. He seemed really happy living near them. Mum just kept herself to herself... she'd wait for dad to come back and they'd be all smoochy in front of us sometimes. I don't know why I'm only thinking of this now. Maybe it's because I'm so old and wise. Tim! Are you still there?"

"Listening to every word," replied Tim. The scraping had stopped.

"Well... I actually had a best friend. He was the only

real one I had as a child. Our birthdays were a few weeks apart and we'd play with dolls in the fields round the back of our houses. We'd throw them up into the trees and shake the trunks until they fell down. There was another family who lived near us with older kids and our parents let us go out with them, for hours sometimes!"

"Is that your embarrassing story?" asked Tim, sounding bemused.

"I'm just getting started," said Melanie. "Wait for it. It's going to shock you and then you might not want to be friends anymore."

"You're such a baby," joked Tim. Melanie loved their banter.

She drew in her breath sharply. It felt like a dream that they were talking like this.

"Are you ready?" she asked. "So… we, that is Danny and I…"

"Danny… I see," said Tim and the scraping started again.

"Yes, me and Danny had a very… bizarre, and very childish fascination of spearing onto twigs and sharp sticks what the many dogs around our neighbourhood often left behind."

"No!" said Tim laughing. "I need to reassess everything now, sorry Mel."

Melanie carried on, feigning insult. "Let me finish now! And throwing it at things – anything we could find. Nothing too damaging, nothing too upsetting for anyone. Trees were actually the main targets, or a small hill. And… cars! Oh my God! Please don't ask me why we did that. It seemed like so much fun at the time. We'd have hours and hours to wander round the estate. But none of the other kids did this, just us. It was our little secret. My mum used to turf me out in the morning and say, 'Come back for lunch if you get hungry!' Maybe she could deal with Saul better with me not around. He was young I guess back then!"

"Maybe in a parallel world to ours, throwing the faeces of four-legged creatures is a completely natural and normal act and is especially expected of six-year olds?" ventured Tim.

"Ha!" said Melanie. "Are you saying I am deranged or something?"

"Yes." said Tim. "Are you done yet?"

"Well, actually no! That is not even the worst part."

"You mean there is something worse than throwing dog crap at people's cars? Go on then," said Tim. "This is already ten times worse than what I was going to tell you."

"You still are!" Melanie said. "Going to tell me, that is! There is no way you're hanging up on me."

The phone went dead and Melanie gasped and put the receiver down. It rang again.

"You are so funny!" she laughed.

"Continue with your sorry tale," Tim said.

"So… one day when we were super bored, we looked for a really white and shiny car. We wanted the perfect target. The whiter, shinier and cleaner, the better! There was an open top car and it was just… sitting there, gleaming in the sun. Oh God, this sounds awful! So we chucked *you know what* at the bonnet and it went flying inside the car."

"You're actually evil Melanie Stoakes. That is horrific! Done?" said Tim.

"No! There's more! By the way, what are you painting?" asked Melanie.

"I am painting… well, I am using a knife… I am scraping the paint and putting the feeling of this conversation into it," he said.

"That sounds… weird… and amazing! Not sure I want to see this conversation! Can I see the painting at some point?" Melanie asked.

"Yes, it's your painting, with your feelings so you can have it when it's finished. So carry on. I want to hear the end of the story."

"OK so we thought we'd run away and then we heard

a knocking from the window near where we were hiding and you'll never guess who was looking out?"

"Who?" said Tim.

"That's right... Mrs Douglas!"

"She sounds like a witch."

"No!" protested Melanie. "She was a really lovely little old lady who grew flowers in her front garden. She made our estate look pretty. Hardly anyone else bothered! She used to always give me little animals like squirrels and owls..."

"Are you making this up now Mel?" asked Tim. "It really sounds like you are!"

"*Shut up*! *Ceramic* squirrels and owls... and a hedgehog. Like the cat George gave me the other day... did I tell you about that? So then of course we had to go to her door and she says... she says...!" Melanie was laughing so much now that tears streamed down her eyes.

"We stood on her doorstep and then said that we'd seen these boys doing it! And there she was, the sweetest, loveliest old woman, standing there with her tortoise-shell rimmed glasses and really, REALLY wrinkly skin. The sound of her knocking on the window had scared the hell out of me as I'd already received my animal of the week!"

Melanie remembered the feeling of shame that had washed over her like a tidal wave. Her thoughts had raced through her mind double speed... *please don't let Mrs. D have seen us. Please, please!* But Mrs.Douglas' face had beamed out like a September sun, warm and glowing.

"She spoke really softly to us, I remember. *'Hello dears!'*" Melanie impersonated her voice.

"*'Now dears, I thought I just saw some young boys putting mud onto that car'...* she'd said. I remember thinking *oh my God, she saw but she doesn't know it was us or what it was... or does she?* We told her, *'They went that way Mrs. Douglas, we saw them, didn't we Danny? Do you want us to see if we can find them? They ran over the hill and by the swings. I think I know where they live...'*"

"So you lied?" asked Tim. "You threw crap at a car and then lied?"

"You know, this isn't the best story I could have told you..." wavered Melanie. "I feel really embarrassed."

"Do you go around throwing crap at cars now, Melanie?" asked Tim, sounding serious now.

'No!" replied Melanie. She noted the change of tone in his voice. "No, not at all, God, of course not!"

"Well, then that happened in the past and you don't need to be ashamed anymore. You were just being a kid. Your parents had shunted you out of the house and you had to make do. Probably because your dad... well, maybe he couldn't cope with you both and that's why you had to stay out so long."

"That sounds harsh," said Melanie feeling annoyed. "I told you that Saul was young back then." She didn't know what to do now. There was a long silence.

"Sorry," said Tim, his voice faltering. "I have a problem with parents letting their kids roam free all day. They lose their rights as parents when they give that much choice and freedom to a child. Don't you think?"

Melanie started to feel really uncomfortable. She was not used to navigating a conversation like this. And didn't entirely agree with Tim either.

"Do you still want to tell me your story?" asked Melanie.

Have I lost a friend that quickly? Her heart started to sink.

"I'm really tired now Mel but listen… why don't we go out soon and we can carry on chatting," said Tim.

"Er... OK," said Melanie but Tim had already put down the phone. She tried to unscramble her brain. She'd blown it!

What was it Mrs Douglas had said to her and Danny?

"Now dears… don't be like those silly boys. Make sure you stay away from mischief."

Melanie tried to back-track the conversation with Tim. He seemed to be blaming her dad for something? She realised that she didn't know anything about Tim's life at all.

I need to give him the benefit of the doubt she thought.

She held her pen above a fresh page in her diary and no words came to mind. What was this feeling? It hurt so badly in the pit of her stomach, in the arch of her feet, even in her chest.

"Just deal the cards in front of you, Melanie," she remembered her dad saying once as the anxiety set in. "Lay them out and deal with them, one card at a time."

Great advice Dad, she thought. *Why couldn't you just lay **your** cards out instead of stacking them up into a giant mountain above your head?*

Her breath was coming faster now and she started to pant, trying to force more oxygen into her lungs. Her throat started to close up as thoughts raced through her head, knocking her brain as they lunged into her, bikes racing around a metal cage, upside down and crashing and falling, falling. She put her hand out to clutch onto something, anything.

You're no good Melanie Stoakes.

Why would anyone want to be your friend?

Not even your dad stuck around to be with you!

*You are **alone**.*

No one loves you.

You don't deserve any friends.

The voices became louder and she felt like she might need to scream to block them out, yet one voice rose higher and stronger than all of them. Melanie held her breath and counted backwards from ten.

"Pel Mel!" her mum repeated up the stairs. "Tim's here to see you!"

CHAPTER 25

RACHEL

Rachel sighed as she folded the last and hundredth towel that day and she was sure she could feel a lump forming in her wrist, a *ganglion* she reckoned. She'd learned this word from her mum who always had one and knew they caused her a lot of grief when they were swollen.

"You've got to bang it *hard* with a Bible," her mum had once said, looking for one in the house even though they both knew they didn't own a copy.

"Why a Bible?" Rachel had asked.

"Because it's a heavy book!" her mum had laughed. The days with hair were definitely slightly better than the days without.

Rachel could hear Sally talking to Melanie in the corridor, prepping her about visiting George. She felt a pang of jealousy as she wished she got on well with Sally too but knew that was probably not going to be the case. She hardly saw her or anyone here for that matter. When the other girls who worked at Sunny Well discovered she didn't smoke, they soon stopped asking her to join them. Except Tracy, who seemed to be around every corner. As if on cue, Tracy appeared out of nowhere, humming and holding a pile of cardboard bed pans. She tapped Rachel on the arm.

"Afternoon, treasure!" she said with a grin that exposed a tooth that seemed to point upwards. Rachel couldn't help but stare and Tracy laughed. "You've spotted my snaggle tooth, I see! If I rub it, I get three wishes! Come on, it can't get any worse, whatever it is you're brooding about!"

Rachel wished that she could just laugh and have a normal conversation but it had been so long since she'd just talked with a friend. Way too long. Although talking with her dad and opening up to him had definitely helped. Tracy looked at her sympathetically. "Look, I'm only going to tell you this, so you can... you know, have a bit of a break now and then. No one will notice or care. There's a broom cupboard just behind you where we store stuff, most of which doesn't even see the light of day. I go in there and sometimes have a nap or read magazines. The light's broken in there but I left a torch if you want it. I've got a big pile of gossip mags in there if you ever need to go in."

"Er... thanks? But I don't think that would be a good idea for me to do that whilst I'm on my work experience." Rachel replied coolly. She looked at Tracy and tried her best to dislike her. Her brain went into overdrive and thoughts habitually started to creep out like a poison.

Her eyes are too small for her face, her back always hunches over and that tooth makes her look like a witch.

Tracy produced two strawberry flavoured lollies from her pocket and offered one to Rachel. "This'll make the hours go faster!" she said, her eyes twinkling.

Rachel felt instantly ashamed. *Wow, I really am a cow* she thought. *What is wrong with me?*

"Um… thanks, Tracy. I…" she trailed off and then took a breath. "I…I don't know if I'm doing any good being here," she added. "Sally's got me folding stuff all day and I don't think she likes me much."

"Oh don't you worry about Sally," said Tracy, puffing her cheeks out and closing one eye. Rachel couldn't help herself and giggled. *She's actually quite funny* she thought. She took the lolly out of the wrapper and started to suck it, feeling like a little girl but quite enjoying this unexpected interaction. Tracy kept on talking, filling in the silence.

"The other girl, Melanie? Well, she seems to have really taken to being here, don't you think? I saw you both on the first day… I hope you don't mind me saying this, but you looked like you hated each others' guts! I reckon Melanie almost seems like a completely different person. And you know what, Rachel? You getting on with all that boring stuff? Don't worry about it. You're doing something good there and you're saving me a big job! It's going to go fast here, you'll see. You're doing OK, kiddo."

Rachel smiled. Tracy couldn't have been that much older than she was. *Maybe this is what it would feel like to have an older sister*, Rachel thought. She was surprised that she quite liked the idea.

"So come on, tell me a bit about yourself!" said Tracy, her smile widening but Rachel was at her social limit. And she didn't want to give too much away. "Maybe later…" she said and threw the rest of the lolly in the bin. Tracy shrugged and smiled and carried on carting the bed pans down the corridor, beatboxing as she walked.

Rachel couldn't help but smile again, or at least she thought her mouth was forming into a smile and then looked around quickly to make sure no-one was looking and slipped into the broom cupboard. She hoped that Tracy wouldn't come back to see she'd taken her advice. The darkness of the cupboard was somehow soothing. She massaged her aching wrist and felt tears come to her eyes. Tracy had been kind to her and she'd been rude back. Or had she? The lines felt so blurred now. She started to think about school and how much she was glad to be out of the routine. Her mum had insisted she ride the bus in the mornings and even though she'd managed to make most people scared of her, she really hated not having the safety of the car anymore. It was noisy and smelly and way too crowded on the bus.

Rachel sank down and rested on the cool floor in the cupboard. She was tired and didn't really want to go back home. She let her mind wander to one particular morning, when the bus had appeared over the crest of the hill as it always did. It would be at least another five minutes before anyone could possibly make their first steps onto the ledge of the bus though as all the straggly, bandy-legged year sevens would clamber on, eager not to miss their registration. Their form teachers bribed them with house points for punctuality which they would receive with delight and so the kids would push even the older ones out of the way to get their place on the bus.

There was also a mad scramble for The Back on the lower deck – such an important place, granted to those who 'deserved' to sit there rather than who got there first. Sometimes, an unfortunate year seven pupil would jump on one of the seats, trying to avoid eye contact with anyone who might be looking their way until some older pupil would yank them up and give them a push down the aisle without so much as a blink of the eye.

This time, as Rachel had boarded and showed her pass to the disgruntled driver, she'd given the lower deck a weary glance as most seats had been taken and trudged upstairs. It was the usual chain of events. Matthew Freemason had tried, as he always did, to save a seat for Rachel and as always, she'd glowered at him and shifted right to the back of the bus, taking up two seats and putting her legs and feet up on one of the girls in her form, usually Mandy Towers who always seemed pleased at this attention from Rachel. As she'd sat down, Rachel had noted an air of expectancy around her. People were grinning and looking really stupid with their lop-sided smiles.

"OK people, what the heck is going on?" she'd demanded feeling slightly unnerved. She'd had her fair share of this in her last school and hoped to God it was nothing to do with her.

Ellis Dunkley had piped up, a little too loudly as everyone had hushed her almost immediately. She'd continued in a voice that sounded like a deranged mouse, she was almost beside herself. Everyone had shuffled forward in their seats, the atmosphere polluted and all eyes fixed towards the opening at the top of the stairs where a boy sat on his own, right next to an open window.

"You know… we thought we'd give a little treat to Freddie Ginger this afternoon… well, you know, he was so mean at school today, telling on us and getting us detention at break!"

Rachel had sighed and thought *who the heck is Freddie Ginger?* She swore she'd never heard of him and then as her eyes scanned the bus, she'd spotted him, Ah yes, Freddie. Ginger was his nick-name. Shock of bright orange hair, arms covered in a million freckles. He'd been breathing on the window, writing someone's name, then smudging it with his hand.

'So… what are you going to do?" she'd hissed, feeling a lump in her throat as she remembered Jonathan from her old school whispering to his friends and pointing at her, making obscene gestures with his hands and whistling.

Ellis had produced an egg from her pocket.

"This!" she'd announced proudly as if she were presenting a golden trophy and she'd smiled so widely that Rachel could see all her teeth, which were startlingly white, gleaming and shiny. Rachel had looked keenly at Ellis and spoke very slowly and carefully with an edge in her voice which most people knew meant *back off.*

"And what are you going to do with this?"

Mark Fleet from the seat behind had suddenly grabbed the egg and said, "Come on! He gets off at the next stop!" Before anyone could stop him, he had hurled the egg straight towards Freddie who'd continued to sit blissfully unaware, listening to the Beastie Boys on his headphones. Rachel had heard someone shouting "Ginnngggeerrrr!" as the egg had traversed over the heads of everyone on the bus, including Freddie and then straight out of his open window and onto someone in the street below. Everyone had burst out laughing, except Rachel and Ellis.

"Why did you try and warn him?" Ellis had ventured, looking a little nervous as to even dare to contend with Rachel. It was then that Rachel realised that she had been the one who'd shouted the warning. She'd blushed bright scarlet, annoyed with herself as she could feel her cheeks stain crimson. She'd pushed Ellis down onto her seat, everyone oblivious as they were still laughing and almost cheering as Freddie still had his ear-phones in and had no idea of his lucky escape.

She'd peered out of the window at the back of the bus and saw a girl waving her hands frantically and shouting and felt a stab of pain in her chest as she remembered Jonathan shoving snow into her mouth. It had been painful. She never forgot that.

The images of the bus started to fade as Rachel's heart softened just a little. The darkness of the cupboard wrapped around her, comforting her. *I am not a bad person* she thought. *I do care. This is the proof. I didn't want that girl to suffer, whoever she was.*

Rachel picked herself up off the floor and slipped quickly back into the hallway. It was so bright and she felt like she'd been gone far too long. Sally bustled around the corner, and almost bumped into Rachel.

"Rachel! There you are! I wondered where you'd gotten to! There are three more baskets of bed linen and flannels in the drying room. Be a love and if you can get them done by the end of the day, that would be grand, thank you!"

Rachel felt her mouth moving into a smile. "Thank you!" she said. And she meant it.

CHAPTER 26

GEORGE

"Hello Melanie, you're a bit late today," Sally said, disapprovingly but with a twinkle in her eye. "You can go straight in to see George today. He's been talking about you. It seems like you are making a big difference. In such a short time too." Sally winked and walked off.

Melanie knocked as she always did and saw that George was fast asleep on his bed, his mouth slightly open and snoring like a softly puffing train. His curtains were closed and his room smelled of medicine and soap. She saw that there were some scattered papers on his desk which looked like latest diary entries. He'd said last time she was there that she could read anything he wrote. *Funny*, thought Melanie. *I see George as much as a friend as I do Tim.*

She looked at the paper and saw that his writing was less tidy and sloped at the end of sentences. She settled down on the floor and started to read, savouring his words.

Samuel reached out to touch the ball, brushing those unforgiving locks out of his face. It kept bobbing out of his grasp. I tried to wade, quite unsuccessfully to the rescue and grab it but it impishly decided to skip away. The wind whipped the silver tops of the waves to lemon meringue foam, the white now engulfing the blue. The blue of Samuel's eyes.

Those big eyes, now widened even more and gazed at me for answers. He wanted the ball. I knew that I had the full responsibility of saving that bit of plastic.

Heroically, I'd thought, I made several more attempts to clutch it to my body but the ball kept moving away, taunting me, creating a nervous tension in the water. My head started to meet the increasing height of the waves and somewhere beyond, I could hear the panicked voice of Mother, reaching, imploring us to return to safe sand. I reasoned with my own panic as the salt started to sting my eyes. The line of the shore moved up and down and when I tried to curl my toes around the milky sand on the seabed, I felt only water, gushing and swirling. I was out of my depth. The other holiday-makers, oblivious to my dilemma, continued to chant, or so it seemed, as their voices blended with the melodies and rhythms of the waves. It felt like warm soup. Soupy water. Imagine drowning in soup. I managed to turn my head for a final glance just in time to see the ball hurtling across the sea and into the distant horizon. Salt from the spray, entwined with fresh tears, brought me back to reality and onto dry sand.

When I arrived back to the shore, scarcely breathing, head full of sea, sand stuck to body, my mother did not know whether to hug or slap me. She did neither at first. My head was cast downwards, the ends of my hair in tendrils, catching the sand.

As I lifted up my face towards Mother, I believe she could see the pain in my eyes. I could see Father behind her, looking furious. She tried her best to shield me. The ball had been a gift from Samuel the year earlier. The memory fades at this point and I catch a flicker of gold and a voice that cuts like a blunt razor... remember George... don't ever forget me...

The voice merges with the sounds on the beach. When thousands of people are making conversation, you only hear a noise, like a thousand bees, the incessant flapping of a million butterflies or hummingbird wings. And there I was, head down, on the sand, looking at the sea, my little body aching from the beating I'd just received from my father, caged within the beauty. Samuel had not been in the sea. Samuel had not even accompanied me on this particular family holiday. He'd gone a long time before. I stared wistfully, longingly out to the ocean, just in time to see the ball gently lift like a feather out of the ocean and into the sky like a soul.

George coughed, waking himself, and saw a young girl standing there reading his notes.

"Hello, Bitsy love," he said, wiping his eyes as they had started to fill up already. He took a drink and then looked again, feeling his insides twist as he saw it was Melanie. "Sorry, love," he said with a sad look on his face. "You honestly do really remind me of my Bitsy. You know, I knew her so well but only for the shortest time really, in the grand scheme of things. I think about what she's doing now, whether she thinks about me or whether she just goes to school and has, what is it they do these days? Have their sleep overs at each others' homes? And eat big boxes of pizza! Every time it's her birthday, do you know what I do?" Melanie walked over to George and sat beside him.

"No, go on. What? Something nice?"

"Well, it's very simple but I just light a candle. I sing happy birthday to her and then I feel a connection to her across those miles… like maybe in that moment, our hearts might be beating in the same rhythm. It's possible don't you think dear?"

"Absolutely," replied Melanie.

George closed his eyes and listened as Melanie spoke.

They took turns to share their stories. He loved to hear Melanie talk. *They had so much in common* he thought.

Melanie continued. "Well, when it was *my* dad's birthday a while back, my mum got all dolled up as if he was going to come out of hospital and take her dancing or something. She put on her favourite spotty dress, the one that has the pleats at the bottom which spin out when she twirls, which is why I figured… you know, the dancing… and she'd done all her make-up. She looked so pretty. Then she sat at the table and just waited. She poured two glasses of fizzy and just… sat there. And then she finally put her slippers on and made a cup of tea. Saul is very attached to mum. He kept on looking in on her in the kitchen then coming back to me to report back. He knew something was wrong and he sat in my room asking me loads of questions that I didn't really know the answers to…"

Melanie broke off and George took her hand and gave it a squeeze, releasing it instantly with a slightly fearful look in his eyes. Melanie continued.

"I don't talk about my brother much, do I? He's only a year and a half younger than me. He's had all sorts of problems and challenges since he was born but my mum, she's fierce around him, I dunno, I guess like a lioness. She decided to teach him herself at home as the schools were rubbish with him. Always testing him, sending him to different schools to see if he'd fit better in there. And then one day, she'd just had enough. We're a bit like twins... except not. He looks quite like me and when people see us together and they don't know us, they think we're the same age."

"Keep talking dear... go on," said George. "Sounds like Saul is a lovely brother. And that mother of yours sounds really wonderful."

"She is..." Melanie beamed. "I mean, don't get me wrong, she does half go on sometimes but... I see how she is with Saul and I see how she was with Dad and she just carries on and on, never stopping, never caring about herself or not seeming to care anyway. We... we don't have much money and she'd always go on at me to get a job. I know I could help more in the house. One day I'll be able to get a good job and help her out. We just don't know what's going to happen to my dad, you know?

"When it was his birthday, I wish I'd lit a candle. That is such a nice idea. They had me when they were really young, you know, my parents that is... like they were only fifteen or something like that. Maybe a bit older. That's my age now! Oh my God! Mum looks older. My dad just looks pretty young... well, he did. I wish I could see him. Coming here to see you, it's helping me but it's hard too.

Not that I don't love coming to talk to you, I really do. But when I talk with you it reminds me of how I could be having these conversations with him. I know it's not long now but I don't really believe he's coming back. I won't believe it until it happens and then I think I'll always be wondering when he'll decide to leave again… or have to."

"Dear, I know exactly how you feel." George noticed that Melanie had tears in her eyes. *What a lot for a young lass to go through* he thought. He then felt a pain in his chest as he remembered his own son.

Did John light candles for his dad, Old George? What if I die in here, a lonely old man with no-one to visit me? It won't be long before Melanie would leave.

He knew that Melanie would soon be leaving as Sally had told him several times, as if he was stupid and couldn't remember. He closed his eyes again and the sound of waves became louder in his head until eventually, he fell asleep, one hand clasping the other, as if to give himself some final comfort.

CHAPTER 27

MELANIE

Melanie was just about to knock on George's door when Rachel walked past her, with a basket of towels. She looked at her and felt a pang of hope. Maybe things could be different here in Sunny Well for everyone. Maybe they could get to know each other?

"Hey," ventured Melanie, feeling brave. "How's it all going?"

"Um… s'ok I guess," mumbled Rachel.

"I didn't think I'd like it here but… I dunno…" said Melanie, suddenly wishing she'd never started a conversation. There was a silence that seemed to go on for ages.

Rachel put the basket down and sat on the floor of the corridor. Melanie looked taken aback, wondering what on earth Rachel was doing. It was weird to see her so close up. She looked different, almost a little defeated. Her eyes were puffy and her skin had broken out in some spots.

"Are you bored of all the folding?" asked Melanie tentatively.

"I'm kinda really liking chatting with George. He's got something called Alzheimer's and it's something to do with memory. I think it's early stages... um... and I don't know if there's something else as well but I don't think he's well."

"I guess," said Rachel shrugging. "I mean, bored of the folding. I actually think it's OK here. It stinks like rotten cabbages... but it's OK. Er... sorry to hear about George. That sucks."

Melanie knew she would be foolish to expect any kind of apology but she wanted to take a chance while she had it. She spoke quickly before she could think about what might happen.

"Rachel... why do you hate me? At school... I just feel like you really don't like me for some reason and I don't know why. Is it something I did?" Melanie felt her hands start to tremble a little and she put them in her pockets. She hoped that George wasn't listening or that Sally wasn't going to rush down the corridor to deal with some bed-wetting emergency.

Rachel's shoulders dropped and she looked Melanie in the eye. "You know, I don't hate you. I just don't... I don't really understand anyone. Or myself! You walk home, don't you? I get the bus... I hate that! It's always some kind of drama.

Maybe I should start walking. We could… we could walk together?"

Melanie couldn't hide her feelings of horror at this suggestion but she tried to be nice.

"Maybe…" she ventured. "But there are some real nutters on the bus! I got egged once on the way back home. I gotta go now, to check on George. See ya."

Melanie wondered why Rachel had opened her mouth wide like a goldfish. *She looks gormless, doing that,* Melanie thought and left Rachel in the corridor. She knocked gently on the door and went in to George's room.

Melanie sat by George's bedside and folded his arms up nearer his pillows so they wouldn't keep flopping down beside the bed. He had his eyes closed and his breathing was shallow.

"George? I've got to go soon. Tell me more about Ellie," whispered Melanie.

"What about heaven though eh? What do you think of it, as a place?" George kept his eyes closed as he spoke. His voice was raspy and his speech slightly slurred and slow. "Do you think we all go there? My dad certainly didn't think so. He was always telling me how I'd be down in hell with him. I asked this question to my dear Ellie once. Would we both go to heaven? We liked the idea of this beautiful place and once, whilst on the beach, we both lay on the sand, side-by-side and peered upwards into the vast-ness of the sky. It seemed to reach out to forever and ever... there was no end, no reachable limit. And that's when we reasoned that heaven definitely existed. We'd make our own hell if we closed our eyes to the sky and didn't see it anymore. What could possibly be more hellish? Samuel had whispered... *what if we were to never know the beauty of the sky again?* As soon as I realised that heaven existed, I felt fine. He would be okay. Ellie ran to my mother and she embraced her... we were all there together you know."

Melanie closed her eyes as George confused his words and memories and remembered how much George loved his dignity.

"George... you told me it was your mother on the beach... that you were young. Ellie wouldn't have been there, would she? Ellie was your wife. And Samuel..."

"Yes, dear..." George muttered. "That's right... I can see them all there now though. I can see them all on the beach..." He closed his eyes again. "Melanie dear... tell me about this boy, Tim."

"Oh..." said Melanie.

"Well... I thought we'd fallen out. We had this conversation on the phone, which was amazing as I don't usually speak to anyone on the phone. And then it got all awkward. I told him a stupid story from my childhood and he found it funny at first… it's so hard sometimes having a friend, don't you think? I thought it would be really easy. It felt easy at first and I felt like I was walking on air as everything flowed…"

Melanie got up to adjust George's pillows and he sighed and smiled. "I'm still here love… keep on talking… Ellie is listening too."

"And then I said something that bothered him. I could hear it in his voice. I felt so… *stupid*, like I'd given too much of myself away too soon. After all, I hardly know him. Anyway, I nearly had a panic attack and…he came round straight away to see me."

Melanie smiled as she remembered.

"He hugged me, as he does, with his big baggy jumper on, even tighter than he'd ever done before. He told me… he told me that his parents used to send him out of the house every day of the holidays and he'd be on his own. He didn't have a Danny like I did. I realised then, that actually I have never been truly alone. I felt so bad George. I always felt so sorry for myself but really, I was just missing my dad. Him not being home was huge, like a big gaping hole. I would say silly things like 'I hate you' but I didn't mean it, ever. I don't know why I said things like that. And I still do. It's like a habit I guess. Sometimes, I'd feel his mood go down as we were talking. He'd be fine one moment and we'd be walking side-by-side and then suddenly, he was there, in that dark place. It was like a cloud had covered his body and he was lost in the mistiness of it all. He must have been in so much pain. It was hard not being able to help him."

Melanie wondered if her dad was thinking about her now.

She was going to see him soon. Was he worried? Nervous? What if he took one look at them all and went back? She missed him so much. And she also didn't want to see him.

George and Melanie sat in companionable silence. Melanie looked at his face; deeply furrowed brow, liver spots and moles mapping his skin. He looked so kind. She wished he was her grandpa. She didn't want him to leave her.

"You know… I wasn't a kind father Melanie," George said eventually, his voice so quiet now that Melanie had to strain her ears to listen. "A bit like Tim's parents perhaps? I didn't feel any connection to him, my John, when he was born. I can't even explain it. It was a strange feeling, knowing you had helped to create such a tiny human but feeling nothing in your heart. When Bitsy was born, I felt all the feelings I should have felt with John. I wonder whether my son thinks of me here now. I know it's all my fault. I should have… I should have made myself hold him. I should have loved him. I should have seen Ellie in him more. Did your dad hold you Melanie? I think he sounds like a wonderful dad... it's just his mind needs a bit of help that's all. We make a fuss about people with broken bones but never when our brains are broken. I think my own father's brain must've been broken. I can see that now. I wish I'd helped John more. I can see now what I needed to do... but it really is too late... and that girl you were talking to outside. Not a friend of yours is she? But it sounds like you both might have a few things in common. Why not take a chance on her, love, eh?"

George drifted off to sleep again, snoring lightly.

"I didn't know that Tim had been so alone as a child,"

Melanie whispered, pulling George's top blanket over him. "Like, really alone. His parents... they never really connected with him. And he didn't connect with anyone. It's a wonder how amazing he is now, don't you think?"

Sally appeared at the door. "Melanie, I think you might need to go and help Rachel for a while. She's got a load of work to do and... it looks like we should leave George for a bit now."

Melanie patted George gently on his shoulder and said the closest thing she knew to a prayer.

"Keep him safe, let him get back to Ellie and his mum and Samuel and maybe even his dad. Amen."

CHAPTER 28

SALLY

Sally called all the staff together at Sunny Well to brief them on the new developments. She noticed Rachel and Melanie sat next to each other, both picking their nails and looking around a bit nervously. They were both equally good in the roles she had put them in. Sally had been very impressed with the way Rachel would focus on the most menial work in the home, never complaining, just continually folding and cleaning and then doing more folding.

"So, today, you know that we have some visitors coming to Sunny Well. And I wanted to prepare everyone for the possibility of…well, we all know that not everyone in here…" Sally found herself struggling to say the words. "We need to be prepared is what I'm trying to say, for every eventuality. Spend extra time with our lovely residents this week as we never know, do we?"

Sally looked at Melanie as she said this, her heart melting. Melanie had worked wonders with George. He'd told her all about Melanie and her life and had never heard him be so animated and open about things. He talked to Sally though now as if she wasn't really there. He kept his focus elsewhere and never gave her proper eye contact. Melanie looked up and nodded knowingly. Sally continued to address her staff.

"Latest news is that we've been awarded extra funding from what appears to be an anonymous benefactor. OK, keep the applause for later. Let me tell you all… that a *very* generous sum of money has been donated and this will mean we can start plans for the complete refurbishment of Sunny Well!"

She saw Melanie look wide-eyed and amazed, and was surprised to see Rachel clapping along with everybody else. There was something special about working here.

Brenda wheeled her chair into the room and up alongside the girls, looking keenly at Rachel.

"I've been watching you dear over the last few days and I have been very impressed. All that work you've had to do! It's a surprise that Sally over here didn't enlist more help for you?" Brenda looked at Melanie who shrugged and smiled.

"Now Brenda, pet, everyone is doing a grand job here," soothed Sally, "and yes, Rachel has really been working well."

Sally was pleased to see Rachel smiling at this praise and even blush a little. She saw the same thing every year.

The young ones came and worked here, grumbling a bit at first and slightly sour-faced and then the magic happened.

"And Melanie has been working with George which is wonderful too," added Sally. "Girls, you don't know how enriching this experience is for you both."

"I do…" said Melanie quickly. "I don't think I've enjoyed myself this much in… well, in quite some time."

She stole a glance at Rachel who looked down at her shoes.

"Well, girls, let's get to it then! Melanie, I suggest you spend a bit of time with George before his visitors arrive and Rachel, you can help me with the lunch today as we have a couple of staff who called in sick this morning. I do hope it's nothing contagious."

Sally went to the staff room to take a few moments to herself. She'd been to see George this morning with the doctor as he suddenly seemed very different. He had lost much of his coherence, his eyes hadn't seemed to focus properly and he was talking to himself more than before. The doctor had talked about George's *motivational reserve* and how his writing and recent frequent chats with Melanie had undoubtedly helped him to keep active and positive whereas in reality he was still also simultaneously losing connections and his brain would keep re-wiring, which would be exhausting.

"Has he been doing anything different recently?" asked the doctor, checking his notes on George.

"The main thing really is that he's been talking… non stop! I listen in the hallways and Melanie, our work experience girl, well she's just fabulous. The way she speaks to him… it's better than we all do here. There is not a single ounce of her that patronises him. She listens to his stories and… and you know what she does? She doesn't just go along with everything he says. And I think in many ways, George has been good for Melanie too. She really reminds him of someone called Bitsy, his granddaughter. He hasn't seen her for years and at first he thought Melanie was Bitsy! Well, George is a clever one and he soon figured it out… I feel that he is, what's the term Doctor?"

Sally looked up expectantly, feeling she'd been babbling as usual.

The doctor looked kindly at Sally.

"It's the calm before the storm," he said. "I see it all the time and you must have seen it too with your line of work? It's… an acceptance. It sounds like he is starting to piece things together in his life, putting the jigsaw together so to speak, with the help of this, Melanie. The fact she resembles someone he loves is very important. But you know, as I said, those connections will happen as much as they are not happening… we never know how it's going to play out.

But really Sally, you know it's more that that. He's stopped drinking as much and he's getting frequent urine infections. One of the reasons why he's increasingly confused is because of that. I think he's made up his mind that it's his time."

Sally stirred her tea absent-mindedly for far too long, gazing into the garden of the home. What was it that John Roody had said on the phone the other day? He didn't really say if there had been an accident or not. Sally thought about the time each year when George would become sad and full of remorse. *Maybe it's a mixed memory* thought Sally. *Maybe he thought he did something terrible, when in fact…*

She put her hand to her mouth and tears sprang to her eyes. She hoped John and his daughter would arrive soon. Melanie had suggested it to her that Bethan should come too. Maybe the pieces of the puzzle would fit together when they came to visit.

CHAPTER 29

RACHEL

The curtains were drawn, the window jammed open with a spoon but still the heat fused in, making Rachel feel as if her skin was wax and that she might melt over her bed if she got any hotter. She peered out of one eye and saw the dust sparkling and dancing in the light. She exhaled hard and the dust motes moved rapidly and randomly in all directions. She thought of the time she'd spent with her dad and wrapped her arms around herself as if trying to keep the memories as close to her body as possible. Being hugged by him had felt... well, like she was small again. She wished she could go back in time. She felt she had done when she'd been in his room.

The heat was unbearable and it wasn't even 10am.

"I could kill for a glass of water," she muttered to herself. Cool. Crystal. Clear. Images of torrential rain and powerful waterfalls infused her brain as she envisaged her head tilting back, her mouth wide open to drink the clear liquid, sliding down her throat, mixing with boiling blood, transfusing through her limbs, refreshing and cool. She put both her hands onto her head and stroked softly as if it were an animal.

"How will I learn to love you?" Rachel asked, her hands circling in soft motions and then sat bolt upright, horrified as she realised her mum was at the foot of her bed, staring at her.

"*Mum*! Can't you knock?" she growled.

Her mum took a deep breath and her voice trembled.

"Rachel, sweetie, shall we go shopping today? It shouldn't be so busy in town as most people will be at the outdoor pool, I reckon. We could… we could eat lunch together and you know, maybe even catch a film?"

Is she for real thought Rachel? Her mum hadn't asked her out since… well, it seemed like forever.

"I dunno…" said Rachel. "I've got work and stuff…"

"Please?" said her mum steadily. "Let's go out today. I need to… I need to spend time with my beautiful daughter." Rachel resisted the urge to think up more excuses. "Sure mum, let me just get ready," she said begrudgingly.

She hopped into a pair of loose-fitting jeans, her favourite blue patterned blouse and dug out white sandals from the cupboard. She brushed the wig whilst it sat patiently on its stand. She heard the words of Johnathan in her head, whooshing and whooping.

You think you're so great don't you? You know what happens to girls like you? Girls like you, never get guys like me. I'm too good for you. I hope all your hair falls out. It'll make you look even uglier than you are now.

Rachel remembered him spitting on the ground beside her and that she'd brought her hands to the little shiny spot on her head. She never wanted to feel that small, ever again.

She stroked the wig on the stand, missing Auntie Joan and wishing it was just easy to hop out of bed and get ready like before. She suddenly stopped and felt excited, her blood pulsing through her veins as if she'd run a mile. It *was* easier to get up in the morning, more than ever! Right? She remembered the words of the specialist.

"You'll have some, what I call 'AHA!' moments Rachel, when the sun will shine and you'll feel glad to be alive and you won't care about your hair."

She'd not believed him of course. And here she was now, feeling like she could suddenly burst. *I'm one of the lucky ones* she thought. Rachel's mind immediately took her to a recent encounter with Tracy at Sunny Well. Sally had told Rachel to get some old rags from the cupboard in the hall to put in the wash and she'd slipped in and shut the door, enjoying the soothing darkness again. She could feel herself changing now that she was away from school.

She felt like a fake most of the time around her friends.

Do I really have any proper friends she'd thought.

People want to hang out with me but it's never real.

She'd reached out and touched what she thought felt like a broom handle, and then heard a noise.

"Who's there?" she'd said sharply, afraid. Her dad had always told her when she was younger that there was no such thing as a monster in the closet but here she was, her heart beating hard in her chest. *Maybe I'm the monster,* she'd thought. *People are always scared of me. No! I have to stop thinking like that!*

"It's me, Tracy," a small voice had said.

"Do you always come in here and spy on people?" Rachel had accused, her tone harsher than intended. She'd sighed. She could hear the way she spoke to people and it always made her body recoil in disgust. She always vowed to be better the next day, then the next and it never seemed to work out. She tried to remember that her and Tracy had already had a bonding moment. *This is what it could feel like,* she thought, *to now work hard to make some kind of connection.*

"Sorry… I just got a little scared. What are you doing in here? There's not even a light on so you can't be reading…" Rachel had said. Her eyes had adjusted to the darkness and she could see that the cupboard was quite big.

"I just needed a break is all," Tracy had muttered miserably. "Things are… they're not too good at the moment. I told you it was a good place to hang out though, didn't I?"

They had both fallen silent for what seemed an eternity. "What's up?" Rachel had said, finally unable to bear the quietness.

"Oh, you wouldn't understand,"

"Well, you don't know that!" Rachel had replied, feeling annoyed. "Try me."

What am I doing here, she'd thought! *Quick, escape! Don't be sucked in by weirdo Tracy.* But there was a little nagging feeling, somewhere in the pit of her stomach that urged her to keep talking.

"Go on…" she'd said, trying to make her voice sound softer. "We're both of us in the dark here. Tell you what, I'll tell you something… something big that I never told anyone before. Then you can tell me, OK?"

Tracy had made a little noise, that Rachel took to mean that she agreed.

"OK, I'll go first."

She'd sucked in her breath and felt her heart start to thump in her chest. "My hair is not real. It's a wig. I have alopecia."

There. She was sick of hiding. Sick of being afraid. Now she'd told Tracy in the cupboard, she could probably go on breakfast TV. She'd laughed at the thought.

Tracy must have moved as something had fallen over making a big metallic clang. They'd both jumped and then started laughing out loud.

"Shhhh! We'll get discovered!" Rachel had snorted.

"Nah!" Tracy had replied. "Everyone knows I come in here and no-one ever bothers me about it. I make sure I get all my work done, mind you. So...I guess it's my turn. And... thank you for sharing. I didn't know that."

"No-one does," Rachel had said. "I hide it well... I think. But it doesn't make me a nice person. In fact, I'm a pretty awful person. Like water that looks like it's crystal clear but really it's poisonous."

"Oh don't say that!" Tracy had said, sounding sad. "That can't be true. Sounds like you've suffered... and when we suffer, sometimes we do things we wish we wouldn't. I'm sure it's not anything to do with your hair, if you really think about it... am I right?"

"Maybe," Rachel had muttered, thinking about her mum and life at home. Was her life really as bad as she made out?

"Well," Tracy had continued, as if Rachel had said something as simple as 'I'm going to buy some bread'.

"I'm taking some time off soon as I need to have surgery on my back. I've had problems with it since I was little but… well, I've had a rough time and the doctor says I've been so tense and lifting my shoulders up, you know… like bracing myself for something terrible to happen. It's kind of developed into a thing now and all the muscles in my back won't release and relax back to normal. Sounds weird… I guess I don't really tell anyone about that."

Rachel had stood there, her feet rooted to the ground. She'd wanted to run but her mind had gone into overdrive, making sure she'd stayed put. She'd listened for the next ten minutes about Tracy being in foster care since she'd been a toddler, shunted from home-to-home and feeling like no-one wanted her. Sunny Well was all she really had in her life now.

"I was quite a difficult child," Tracy had continued. "which is why no-one could really put up with me for too long."

Her voice had sounded so sincere and sad in the darkness. Rachel had always seen Tracy dancing and singing through the corridors in Sunny Well, joking with the residents and always trying to make people smile. Rachel had suddenly wondered what would happen if she continued to work here, just on Saturdays and maybe in the holidays. She'd then be able to maybe just be there a little, for Tracy.

Wow, if I'd known all I needed to do was stand in a dark cupboard a few times to get a bit of life perspective, then I could have done it a lot sooner, she'd mused and smiled to herself.

Rachel's thoughts were interrupted as her mum called from downstairs. She felt the wig again. It *had* been defining her way too much. She couldn't believe her mum had asked her to go out. It felt like a dream. *Imagine if I just left the wig here for a while...*

"No more hair wash night!" enthused Rachel, catching herself in the mirror. "Braiding by Mum on a Saturday morning before horse-riding class? Not any more! Trying to fit my wig in a cap for swimming class? No way! Mum nagging me, asking if she can brush my hair before school? Never again!"

She smiled at herself. "Yeah Rach, this feeling isn't going to last but make the most of it."

She picked up her wig and addressed it solemnly.

"Do you know what?" she said. "I think that we are going to take a little break from each other."

She grabbed her sunhat and went downstairs to meet her mum.

CHAPTER 30

JOHN

John Roody stood at his father's bedside, and bowed his head. Bethan stood beside him, her eyes fixed on her grandfather's face. Someone coughed at the door and they both turned round.

"Melanie...?" said John. "Melanie!"

He awkwardly tried to embrace her, which ended up as a clumsy hand-shake as she slightly stepped back. He could feel blood rushing to his cheeks. *Man up* he thought. *No, those are not my words* he corrected himself.

"Melanie, I've been told that you've been instrumental in helping my dad recently. I want to… I really want to thank you."

It was on the tip of his tongue to also say *sorry, sorry that I treated you so harshly at school, sorry for not noticing your pain and sorry… for everything.* Melanie looked at him and smiled wryly.

"It's OK," she said. "It's been really great to get to know your dad. Old George they call him here! I just call him

George. He's a real character. He's been writing loads these last few years although mainly repeated diary entries. I've read so many of them. He's got a lot of lovely memories about his late wife… um… your mother. But… well, since recently, he's been writing a lot more. Some of his words are confused but I think… I think you'd find them to be comforting."

"John?" George sat up in bed, rubbing his eyes as if in a dream. "Bitsy?" he added incredulously and tears streamed from his eyes. Bethan and John came close to his bed.

"Dad," John choked, full of regret and relief that he'd caught him in time. He looked at his dad's face, lined and etched with unfamiliar wrinkles. His heart sank as he realised how much time had passed.

"Dad… please forgive me. I am so, so sorry."

He turned to Melanie. "I am really sorry," he mouthed to her and then turned back to George.

"I have so much to tell you, Dad!"

Melanie crept out of the room before George could see her.

She'd already said her goodbyes to him.

They all spoke for hours, George flitting in and out of consciousness. Sally had made sure that George was as comfortable as possible, putting out extra chairs for his guests and a box of tissues. She'd put fresh daisies on the desk, a flask of tea and a plate of shortbread biscuits. She did this for every resident whose family came to visit them in their last days. Some didn't get there on time. John put his head close to George's and read an extract from his diary, saying, "Dad! You've got a real way with words.

Listen to how beautifully you write.

I was in the garden with dear Ellie in my dreams last night. It all felt very real somehow. Every time she spoke, I could see birds, crystals and musical notes flowing out of her mouth. It was like she was speaking the language of beauty. It was autumn in my dream and the leaves carpeted the ground in soft patterns, warm reds, yellows and browns, the trees swaying and bowing to each other in the twilight breeze where they spoke to one another in a language unknown to man..."

John's mouth started to tremble and felt that if he continued, an actual dam might be released from his whole being. He passed George's words to Bethan, who cleared her throat and read as her teacher had taught her, slowly and with great expression.

"I could hear the gentle rippling of a nearby stream, enclosed and guarded by the trees, the tops of which were so tall, they gracefully brushed against the blackening sky. The melody of a stray bird, abandoned by its family, flew earnestly in search of warmth... I asked the earth to calm me down, to take me to its realms so that my soul may soar to the heavens. Ellie, I am ready... I am ready...

"I never knew Grandma, did I?" Bethan asked. "It's been so long Dad, since I saw Gramps... I don't really feel I know him now either."

Bethan started to cry.

There was a knock at the door and Sally came in, motioning for Bethan and John to come into the hallway. Melanie stood there, her eyes low to the ground, trying to muster as much respect for them all as she could.

"Bethan, Bitsy...!" said Melanie. "George wanted me to have this but I think it should belong to you now. You know, he talked about you a lot. He loves you both so much... and is so full of regret." She put the little ceramic kitten into Bethan's hand.

Melanie looked at John and he could hardly believe they were all here, in Sunny Well.

"Melanie," John started. "I really don't know what to say. I must tell you though... I've handed my notice in. We're..." he looked at Bethan. "This young one wants to move in with me and we're…er, trying to see what's possible, you know, through the courts."

Melanie took a breath and even though she was still wary of him, she turned to face John, trying to make sure her voice didn't wobble when she talked.

"Mr Roody… it's been amazing to be with your dad these last few days. I wasn't looking forward to going back to school but… I think it is all going to be OK. I really do."

She left the room and John and Bethan held George's hand through the night, telling him stories, all their news and their joys and their woes, telling him that they loved him.

"Dad… I never did get the chance to properly tell you… you know that day you accidentally ran over Bethan's bike? I am *so* sorry that Denise screamed at you the way she did. She was just really scared that something had happened to Bethan. I know she didn't get on with you as well as we'd all hoped, well, water under the bridge, as they say, eh? Sally, lovely nurse she is, told me that sometimes you'd get a bit confused and think you'd hurt Bethan in some way."

John was breathing fast, trying to get his words out as quickly as he could before it was too late.

"But you never did hurt me, Gramps," added Bethan, holding George's hand as tight as she could. His eyes remained closed but his face transformed into a smile and he squeezed her hand.

The sun started to rise and they could hear the birds sing their early morning chorus as George breathed once, twice and then… he was gone.

CHAPTER 31

MELANIE

Dear Diary,

My thoughts are wandering. Waiting for Tim. Not knowing what's going to happen. I want to feel like it's all going to be OK. It's almost as if I have no control over what enters my mind. I often lie on my bed at night, looking upwards to the zillion stars, moons and plastic planets that illuminate my ceiling. They were the perfect idea (my idea I might add) for me to lose myself in my favourite day-dreams. I can't believe he's gone... like a lantern rising to the eternal sky... Wow, I sound like George!

Melanie let the pen hover over the paper, wanting to write something beautiful and poetic, waiting for Tim to arrive. Everything she wrote now sounded wrong, and a bit pathetic, like she was trying too hard.

"Be authentic..." she heard a voice. "Just be you. Write your feelings, your stories..."

"Hey Tim," said Melanie, as he came up behind her. He sat on the swing next to her and they swung, back and forth as a new wind started to pick up some of the grass that had just been cut, sprinkling it over the park like old memories.

"Melanie... I'm sorry," said Tim.

"Why?" Melanie asked. "You haven't done anything wrong. If anything, I need to learn how to be around people a bit better! I think I made a bit of a fool of myself the other day..."

"No," protested Tim. "That's just it! You didn't. I told you that I had therapy once right? I don't really know how to be with people... I honestly don't. I've never actually had a proper friend Mel. Yeah, sure, I'm always surrounded by people at school but true friends? I have a feeling that you might just be my first one!"

"For real?" Melanie asked, a smile sparking on her lips. "A friend who happens to also be 'lovely'?" she added.

They both laughed.

"Let's walk, come on," said Melanie and they did their usual circuit around the estate, sitting down on kerbs, laughing, talking, sitting in silence.

"Tim, do you feel ready to tell me about, well, about anything?" asked Melanie. "I feel like I've gone on a bit about myself but what about you? What's your story?"

"I don't really have one!" said Tim. "*My* story is the most boring one of all. Nothing happened in my family! No death, no illness… just… well, nothing! I grew up. My parents kept themselves to themselves and I was outside a lot of the time, just thinking, doing my own thing. They did me a favour. I've day-dreamed novels and poetry books… one day I'll become a famous writer! Or an artist! I get so much inspiration for so many creative things, sometimes I feel like I can't choose between them. It really sucked that for GCSE, we could choose only one thing from art, music and drama. Anyway… I just reckon that all that thinking time actually really helped me. I dunno exactly what I want to be but it needs to be something creative. Wow, did I have plenty of time to get my brain bored when I was younger! Throwing a tennis ball against the wall and catching it, for hours! Walking to school on my own even when I was little.

Eating alone at the dinner table as my parents would eat way after I went to bed. But yeah… they did me a favour.

"My mum had this weird thing… Every night before bed, she'd give me a big hug and say that she loved me. That sounds like a normal mum thing, right? But to me, it felt… impersonal though, like it was a ritual for her. Something she *had* to do, not something that she really liked doing. I never saw much evidence of her loving me but… well, you never know. I'd like to believe that someone did. We went on summer holidays but I'd always be put in the section for the kids, you know, the awful campsites where you have to sing songs all day long, learn circus skills and throw custard pies at clowns," Tim shuddered.

"It feels strange," he went on, "to think that my parents don't really know much about me. As soon as I turn sixteen, I'll be gone. I don't know where but, I don't fit in with them. They don't understand me."

"Are you sure it's not just a teenage thing?" Melanie asked, shielding her eyes from the sun which had been hiding in amongst the clouds and was now shining fully on them both.

"Yeah, I'm really sure. I don't know what everyone else's deal is… but I really don't get why my parents had me. Or why they didn't put me up for adoption. I thought school would be a haven for me in many ways but it was worse. People have always thought I was a bit weird." Tim grimaced and Melanie took his hand.

"But I always thought you were so popular. You seemed to have so many friends," insisted Melanie.

"You just saw what you wanted to see," said Tim with a lopsided smile. "Appearances can be deceiving. No one knew what I was ever really thinking… I do wonder if I know myself sometimes! Maybe life isn't as bad as it seems either. And maybe weird is good?"

"Weird *is* good," said Melanie. "I feel like I'm a bit weird too. Maybe it doesn't mean what everyone seems to think it does. You can tell me more if you want. Or not... "

Tim's eyes glazed over as he took a trip into his memories. "There was this one time, the boys in the class stole the skipping ropes from the girls and made a ring around me in the playground. Not just one or two kids, all of them. I was in the middle and they kept on skipping up to me then skipping away. I kept trying to leave the ring but they kept knocking me back... things like that happened a lot at primary school. I tried to make up games to play, you know, so that people would look at me and think I was doing something... purposeful? But I don't think the kids were fooled. No one ever got into trouble. I never had bruises you see... just these ones up here." Tim tapped his head and sighed. "I often felt like and well, still feel that maybe I just imagined it all. Maybe the kids were actually not too bad and I was too sensitive? Maybe I wasn't lonely and it was all in my head?"

"Well, you feel how you feel," said Melanie. "And I totally relate to what you said. I wonder how many notes I wrote for my diary whilst at school... half of them were to make me look like I was doing something else. Seems like a million years ago now. I wish I could get rid of all that for you! Or at least I wish I'd been in your school... we would have been best friends for sure. No-one would have touched us."

Tim smiled wryly. "That would have been nice. Now, I just can't wait to get out of this place," he said. "As soon as I can, I'm out of here. But Mel... I *will* stay in touch with you. You've been... really brilliant. I love you for that."

Melanie hugged her knees as she always did and felt like her smile might fall off her face.

"Being with George really taught me something," she said. "He had all these memories of when he was younger but so many of them kept crossing over and changing. He couldn't keep hold of some of them. He didn't talk about his dad too much but I think he had a pretty rough time. He told me... he told me about Roody too. He said he'd been a really awful dad to him. But in all the time I was with George, I just felt I was in the presence of a really sweet man. And in that time, he was. We can all change. We can all make new memories. My dad... I know it's not going to be easy for me when he comes back... probably even less so for him. I don't want him to get old like George and be full of regrets. I missed my dad, well, still do but I was also getting used to him not being around. Oh my God that sounds awful! Hey, we could always adopt you, you know! Saul would love a brother!"

Tim laughed then reached into his bag and grabbed a scroll that was tied with a hair band.

"It's not awful, what you're saying about your dad. It's normal to feel that way. How else are you supposed to feel? I'm guessing you didn't plan for your own dad to be ill and for him to get himself help, which just happened to take more time than you wanted. Anyway… changing the subject! I used to keep a dream diary…" Tim said.

"Lame!" replied Melanie flicking his arm then resting her head on his shoulder. "And yeah, thanks about my dad. I guess you're right. Tell me about your little dream diary!"

"I kept a book by my bed and would wake in the night and write down my dreams, to the letter. I'd have really vivid, colourful ones that were more like complete stories. Sometimes I'd wake up and remember every single detail, other times, the logical order of the story would escape my mind but would return to me in, like fragments you know? In one of them, I was standing on a cliff-side and kept having flash backs of being in a cave. It was dark and the stench in the darkness was so overpowering. I was trapped in the stomach of a beast of some sort and even though it had digested me and in effect, put me to my grisly end, I was still alive and I knew, in my dream-state that there was someway I could escape the growling stomach where masses of other captured individuals were kept, half-alive and waiting for the knowledge of their fate. Every time the monster opened its jaws, I was aware of the brightness outside. I could smell the sweetness and freshness of the air and I could see a light so intense yet so soft and beautiful…"

Melanie went silent and squeezed his arm. "That sounds horrific," she murmured.

"Mel… you're that something beautiful for me. I appreciate you so much. I'm so glad I called you that day. I was horrifically nervous. More so because I didn't want you to think I was asking you out. OK now that sounds really rubbish! Do you want to see your painting?" asked Tim.

He unravelled the scroll and laid it out in front of Melanie, holding the ends so they wouldn't bend upwards. As first it looked like a mess of colours but as Melanie looked closer, she could see textures, layers, clouds floating in forms of birds, wandering musical notes that looked like thoughts and amber-coloured eyes that fell from beautifully spiralling black trees like leaves in the autumn. She gasped.

"Tim, this is wicked! I love it so much. It's like you've captured exactly who I am. This is me! In weird abstract painting form! You should have an exhibition or something!"

"Well," said Tim, "that is something I could probably do! Do you want to help me get some paintings together and I reckon I could find a space in the library in town? Or in that new veggie coffee shop down Bridge Street? What's it called? The Laughing Lentil? I keep hearing that it's got a pretty cool vibe going on there. I just need a space where they've got a lot of white walls that would look great with some abstract messed up artwork!"

Melanie hugged Tim tightly and felt the strange pounding of hope in her heart, like a distant beating drum. He looked really excited and she could feel a change in his energy. She breathed in the smell of his jumper, wishing she could take away the pain and sadness from his earlier years, wishing she could shield him from his future, wishing she could be with him forever but knowing that they were just friends. Would that change in the future? She wasn't sure about anything right now, except that she felt really good in this moment.

"I know Mel," Tim said as if reading her mind. "And for the record... we're not just friends, we're the best of friends."

CHAPTER 32

RACHEL

The two weeks at Sunny Well had sped past and it was time for the girls to leave. Rachel was glad it was all over although the prospect of going back to school was a bit daunting. She wondered whether to change her wig and give her class-mates a shock. Maybe she didn't need to hide anymore. She felt lighter, more free.

Rachel was being dropped off first, so she turned to Melanie and gave her a smile, a proper smile this time. Melanie gave her a look in return that said, *no worries* and this was enough. *Not the happy ending I'd expected* Rachel thought and couldn't help but grin. *Maybe it just doesn't have to be that easy.*

"Melanie!" she called as she got off the bus. "I… I've got something for you."

Rachel fumbled in her bag. "I didn't really know the right time to give this to you. We might not see each other at school so… maybe this is the best time."

She folded a piece of paper into Melanie's hand and

then gave her a little wave and walked up the path to her house. It felt good to do something nice. Maybe she could even start making a habit of it. She'd gone into George's room when everything had been packed away and his bed lay bare. She'd felt a twinge of regret that she hadn't been part of that journey, like she had missed out on something really special. She'd looked at the room, all sparse, thinking of how much time Melanie had spent in there. She'd noticed that the bin needed emptying so she thought she'd do one last job before leaving. Then she'd spied the bit of paper sticking up at the top with Melanie's name on. *I'm going to do something nice* she'd thought. *Wow, it's that easy!*

Rachel watched the mini-bus go down the road and sighed with relief. It had been a lot of work. She went straight to her dad's den and opened the door to the cage. The birds stayed put but it made her feel better. Her dad had told her that she was welcome anytime in there so she felt it was a den for both of them now. She remembered Brenda's kind words and smiled. She definitely wanted to go back to Sunny Well, if they'd take her on. That had surprised her. Go back? Maybe there was a chance that she could make a friend after all. She had been impressed at how brave Melanie had been to talk to her. It was as if it had broken down a wall of defence she'd spent so long building up.

She thought about her shopping day with her mum. It hadn't all gone exactly to plan and there had been lots of tears, mainly from her mother, of course. There had even been one moment when they'd bumped into someone from her mum's work, who'd looked at Rachel in her sun hat and exclaimed,

"Did you have your hair all cut off Rachel? That's a shame, it was so pretty."

The friend had turned to Rachel's mum and then had carried on, "Why do the young girls do this to themselves these days... it's a wonder, it really is."

Rachel had whipped her hat off quickly and fanned her face with it. Her mum's face had actually turned as red as a pillar box and the friend had almost fallen over backwards, not able to utter a single word.

"It's all the rage now, isn't it mum? In fact, we're going to the hairdressers now, to get the same for her. Aren't we?" Her mum had looked shocked at first then laughed nervously.

"It's OK!" Rachel had said as the friend hurried away. "Maybe... just maybe we have to laugh about it a little bit more. I've had a lot of time to think recently and it struck me. I am not sick. I have all my limbs. My internal organs all work. I just don't have hair. I'd rather lose all my hair forever than, oh I don't know! I am stronger than you think. Mum! Please… just touch my head. Don't be scared."

Rachel had put her mum's hands on her head. "It's just how when I was born… well, not really as I was a freaky, hairy baby, right?" Her mum had laughed.

They'd eaten lunch in the new expensive restaurant in town and her mum had over-ordered so there had been a feast on the table. She'd kept crying, then laughing and Rachel felt that even though her mum was a mess, she was her beautiful mess. Rachel knew she had much more to say and she'd gone over what she wanted to say a thousand times but it always sounded weak.

Come on Rachel, you're stronger than this she'd thought, digging her finger nails into the palm of her hand so hard they'd made marks. This might be her only time to break through a bit and have some real honesty between them.

"This is all I ever wanted, Mum," Rachel had said. "I don't care about my hair… well I do, but what I care most about is just… doing more with you! We never hang out anymore. I see leery Sam from next door more than I see you. By the way, can he just stop coming round from now on? He makes me feel really uncomfortable."

Rachel's mum had suddenly looked serious and grasped her daughter's hand.

"Yes, yes, of course! Now, listen love, I wanted to bring

you out today… it was, important. I hope you won't kill me but… I read the letter that you wrote to Joan."

"Mum!" Rachel had roared, horrified, and several customers had looked up, startled. "Don't you have any idea about privacy? That was something *personal!* I gave it to Dad to put in the post! How on earth did you get it?"

Her mum had looked at the people staring, then smiled nervously at her daughter. "Well… me and your dad had a *really* big talk. It was *not* pleasant I can tell you! I know that man loves me but… well, I needed to hear some of the things he said to me. And he told me you'd asked him to send the letter and I told him I wanted to read it first. I know I shouldn't have done that! But I felt desperate Rachel. I wanted to get some kind of insight… and I did! It was about time I took charge and found out a bit more about you. You're important to me. I might not have shown that a lot lately… or at all… but you really are."

She'd looked to the back of the restaurant and smiled and waved at someone.

"Look behind you love… she flew in just last night. She got your letter and we arranged straight away for her to come. She'll be here for only a week mind you, then she'll be back to her wacky lessons in the bush."

Rachel had squealed as she saw Joan standing there with a wide-brimmed hat perched on her head and an all-in-one trouser-suit, looking exquisite as usual and had rushed over to give her the biggest hug of her life.

"Now, this is the not the wig we bought for you, young lady, is it?" Joan had said, eyeing Rachel's hat with mock disgust. "Let's all go to London tomorrow and get you a whole load of them! You can choose any colour and style, my darling. I got your letter! You are one brave cookie I can tell you that now!"

Rachel had sat back and watched her mum and her aunt hug each other and drink tea. *Things could change in a moment,* she'd thought. *It takes one conversation, one letter, one brave step… that is all it really takes. It must have taken a lot of guts for my mum too…*

Rachel's dad popped his head round the door of the den, interrupting her memory flow. She jumped and laughed.

"You gave me a fright, Dad!" she said.

"Did you see? Look!"

Rachel's dad pointed and she saw that one of the birds was pecking around the window.

"The little fella could only do that because you enabled him to. It was his choice in the end… but you opened the door. Well done, lass!"

Rachel smiled and went to get her mum to come and join in. It was as if a spell had been broken.

CHAPTER 33
MELANIE

"PEL MEL!" yelled Angela up the stairs. "Come on! You're going to be late!"

"Coming!" Melanie hollered. "One sec!"

"And you've got a visitor!" her mum added impatiently.

Melanie sat at her desk and folded the paper in half with tears in her eyes. She'd just read a letter. One that she would treasure forever.

Dearest Melanie,

John, my son was a real wonder and he is going to write this down for me. I bet he is really annoyed as I am saying about three words to the minute. But I think it is important to write to you. I know that my time is nearly at an end. Funny as I feel like I could run and skip and hop now! It's all in my mind though. My body is definitely saying enough is enough! But I am ready to go. I have said my goodbyes and made my peace. And you, dear one were a big part of that. I shall be forever grateful for your friendship, your humour, your honesty and your appreciation of me. Thank you for sitting with me all those times and listening to me warble on. I really do go on don't I! When you see birds, think of me. And I will be thinking of you. There are a lot of people waiting for me I know.

I am sure we will meet again but for now, enjoy your life and make the most of it all. Don't bear a grudge for too long dear, because we all know how that can turn out eh? Remember to forgive, before you forget. And keep writing your diary because my diary helped me to keep all my memories alive even if some of them might have been a little bit jumbled and back to front.

Signing off now and you make sure you spend some good time with your dad. He needs you as much as you need him.

God bless,

George

Melanie ran down the stairs skipping the last two and landing with a jump in the hallway. Her hair was neatly twisted in a bun and she had cream blush on her cheeks and a simple swift black line on each eye, uniform ironed, on and ready to go. She swung by the kitchen to hug her dad tightly who was nursing a cup of milky tea with one hand

and ruffling Saul's hair with another. Melanie made every effort to take in this scene. It was so special. Her dad's hair was all over the place and he had a pair of pyjamas on with little green aliens flying around in spaceships. It looked so normal, him sitting there, like he'd never been away. His eyes looked distant but happy. Her heart thumped a little in her chest and she took a deep breath in and swallowed the feeling of panic that always bubbled underneath. She wanted to stop thinking of the 'what ifs' and just be in this moment, just this once.

"Look Saul!" Melanie proudly showed her brother the embossed logo that read *Sunny Well Staff Help* sewn onto her t-shirt. He laughed, his mouth stuffed full of toast with peanut butter, his new favourite.

"The word *Sunny* is on your BOOB," he giggled. Melanie playfully swiped at his head and gave him a hug.

"So how long are you volunteering for, Baby Beet?" her dad asked.

"Just a two-week stint, then they'll choose a couple of us to stay on as Saturday staff – paid! Here's hoping they choose me! Rubbish pay but still! Can't wait! See you all later." Melanie hugged her dad and gave Saul another tight squeeze, grabbed her jacket and opened the door to see Tim leaning on the wall outside.

"Wanna walk with me today?" he said. " I'll be working

at the factory round the corner for a double shift this week, packing... wait for it... cardboard boxes into more cardboard boxes. Will be better than shovelling pizza toppings onto cardboard pizza bases, mind you," he said and they headed down the back hill to take the longer route to the home.

"You know, Rachel volunteered too?" said Melanie. "I was so surprised. But I'm glad, you know? It's been a funny few weeks. Working there has been… good! It's really helped everybody. Oh by the way, funny thing... my dad just called me Baby Beet! After all this time and he is still calling me cute food names. I really love it though... it is SO great to have him back. Weird, but great weird."

Angela called out after her daughter as a stray piece of paper whisked out of Melanie's bag and fluttered in the wind outside the house but it was too late. Melanie and Tim were deep in conversation. She smiled as she thought of her daughter having a good friend. She couldn't help but cast her eyes downwards to the paper and enjoyed seeing the scribbled handwriting.

Dearest dear Diary! For later… add this to proper diary!

It's back to school and I am sitting here on the steps of the music block watching the gaggle of girls get up to their usual tricks. Can you believe, Rachel Shill just looked over to me and nudged her head my way as if to say 'Come on over'. Not today Rachel... but this is it, isn't it? Moments like this can happen. One moment, I am sitting here and feeling like the worst person on the planet and today, I can feel happy. I am alive. I'm not stupid though. I know that tomorrow, Saul will be winding me and mum up and it's probably going to be a down day for dad soon. He's so different since he got back, but in a good way.

I love my dad and I'm pretty sure that he is always going to be on medication. But he's my dad and I am SO proud of him for taking himself somewhere where he could get better. It felt like forever when he was away but now he's back... it's just like normal again, whatever that means.

I looked at Tim the other day and my heart stopped jumping around like it was trying to escape from my chest. He's OK, but I don't like him like that. Makes me laugh when I thought he was drop dead gorgeous. I mean, he is but NOOOOO!!! This is going to sound sad and soppy but he really is the best friend I could ask for right now. I LOVE the record that he gave me to listen to. Mum helped me get a second-hand record player for dad so I made us both a cup of tea and we sat down and listened to the whole album in silence. I felt I was completely lost in it. They're called The Stone Roses... my absolute new favourite band. I love how their music makes me feel. And I love that I could share that with Dad. He really loved it too.

Me and Tim are going to visit George's grave together tomorrow. I hope that Sally will come. And my mum... Mum! I hope you're not reading your daughter's diary! But as I know you won't be able to resist... I love you. You are my rock and my strength. I look up to you so much. Thank you for teaching me how to live in this world and survive. Thank you for staying with Dad. For teaching me that it's not always easy... but that we can, what was it you said once when Dad left? We can choose to make our way to the eye of the hurricane, or get swept away with the storm like everyone else. You're one in a million Mum and I know I hardly ever say it but I'm glad you're in my world. Now quit reading my personal stuff!

*** Add more notes in about weekend when it happens and how I felt when I saw Sean at school today... SWOOOONNN!

Angela put the paper on Melanie's desk and went downstairs to get the breakfast table cleared away before work. Life was not great and it was not bad. It was in the middle and that was just fine.

CHAPTER 34

ROBERT

Robert waited until he heard the door shut then he breathed a sigh of relief. He was home right now. Home. What did that word mean? He felt comfortable here, with the sounds at breakfast and the smell of the washing hanging on the radiators. When he looked in the cupboard and saw his favourite mug, he felt thrilled inside, like he was seeing an old friend.

Robert walked through the house, savouring each room. It was strange to have no noises around. This wasn't where they'd always lived but he kept seeing familiar things, like a photo, a picture drawn by Saul, a book that he'd read a thousand times to Mel when she'd been tiny. He saw the paint peeling off the walls and he felt guilt wash through him. Did he deserve to be here, back with his family? They certainly had seemed really happy to see him.

How did he feel? He wasn't sure. His heart felt full of love and also empty. He felt full of hope for their future but also that it would be bleak and a bumpy, maybe even impossible ride. A few months ago, he'd lain in his bed, missing everyone and he'd suddenly felt an awful feeling. What if he could never leave here? He was able to... could have walked out the door any moment he wanted. But... what if he just couldn't go back to his family? Maybe that is how it was always going to be. Always wondering, always a little lost. Maybe he was always going to feel like this. His therapist had said that it would be helpful if he mapped out what he wanted from life, wrote down every day the things he was grateful for and continued with the therapy, going to weekly counselling sessions.

Robert got his bag and riffled through receipts that were already starting to pile up and made a mental note to put them in the bin later on. He remembered Melanie calling him to the lounge, putting the needle on the record then the music starting. It was unlike anything he'd heard before. It made him feel like things could really get better. He smelled marzipan when he heard the singer, crooning about *wanting to be adored* and his chest heaved as if he couldn't get enough of the melody in his soul.

Maybe that's really what this is all about he'd thought. *We all just want to be loved in some way.* The way his kids had looked at him when he'd met them at the door... it would stay with him forever. He thought they would hate him. How on earth had they been so happy to see him? Melanie had hugged him and wouldn't let him go. He couldn't breathe. Saul had almost run him over, like he'd only gone out to get a pint of milk and a paper. Good old Saul! That kid! And Angela... oh she'd been a sight for sore eyes.

"You did the right thing..." she'd whispered in his ear. "But we are SO glad you're back, Rob."

She'd then got on and made dinner, which was classic Angela. He loved her for that.

He got his old leather-bound diary out of the drawer. He'd bought two for the price of one and had given Melanie one in the hope that she'd start writing. Writing was his happy place, somewhere to order his thoughts, somewhere for him to escape. He hadn't even looked at it the past year though. He felt the leather in his hands and brought it to his face and breathed it in. His hands itched to start writing. He thought Mel was a lot like him, which half-delighted him and half-scared him to death. He thought of Saul for one moment... Saul! That boy's face was almost always wreathed in smiles. He definitely took more after Angela. Robert grabbed a pen from the table and started to write.

I guess the whole of humanity is on a constant voyage. We all crave something, some destination, with stops on the way, the ability to sightsee. I sometimes feel that

I spend far too much time mulling over my past. Distorting it even. Re-arranging events to suit me. I have moments of reflection, of utter joy and happiness, then I am flung violently to the depths of a well, one that is deep, with a spattering of water at the bottom, stagnant, and I am unable to move.

The narrow well is steep, with slimy walls like a monster's tongue. I try to make my way up and out of the well. I manage to fit my giant feet and hands into tiny crevices, which offer some degree of support... Then I slide steps downwards and the light at the opening becomes increasingly distant.

Will I make it to the top in time?

In time for what though?

This, I constantly ask myself.

What is it that I am trying so hard to achieve?

Through analysing my past and all the events which led me here, perhaps I can achieve the sense of happiness that poets write about and dreamers dream of. In my mind, I can see the crevices, small, yet inviting, welcoming... I need to decipher where in my life those crevices are. I need to hold onto what I have.

I have Angela, Melanie and Saul. I know I love them. I know I am grateful for them. Sometimes, when the sun is not shining, it's hard to see the world beyond the shades of dulled colour and grey. I need to find a way to remember that even if the sun isn't blazing on my skin, it's still there, behind the clouds, giving the world life and light, shining on everyone, including me. The sun is always there but we can shut ourselves away in our own darkness... we can remove ourselves from the warmth of its rays yet the light continues to shine and is always there, ready to be accessed, ready to be enjoyed and savoured, even in the reflection of the moon. I know already that I am strong, I am one of the survivors. I now need to work on thriving and living my life, seeing my kids grow up and loving them so they can live and love their lives.

Robert put down the pen and picked up the phone to call his therapist.

"I'm ready to make a plan," he said.

Never the End...

ACKNOWLEDGEMENTS

Thank you for reading *Little Birds in Cages*. It took a long time to write and even longer to get it published! What a journey! So many steps and so many people involved. I would really like to thank first and foremost, my husband Tom and our two wonderful daughters, Maya and Willow, for supporting and encouraging me the whole way through! I love you all so very much and feel blessed every day to have you in my life.

I would like to thank Erica for her brilliant type-setting, formating and working on the book to make it look awesome!

Thank you to Charlie, Alex, Bridie and the coolest peeps at Ordinary Toucan for the beautiful cover. I love it with all my heart!

And thank you to the team at The Lighthouse Agency for editing the story and giving me fantastic tips and encouragement to shape it into the book you have in your hands today.

Sending hugs to my cheer-leading and supportive rock of friends and family: Mama Bear, Dad, Mum, Matthew, Emma, Fleur, Minnie, KatKin, Jay, Hannah, Vincent, Faizi, Sunray, Fariborz, Natasha, Andrew, Soo, Jordan, Yasmin, Wendi, James, Tara, Nikki, Krista, Rob, Jenny, Stephen, Rita, Margie, Enis, Kimberly Sis, Hazlet, Selina, Maria, Barney, Hari, Pamela and the Douglai, Fiona, Jules, Jo, Meeks, Liz, Serena, Joy, Roxana, Annabel, Heather, Ramin, Tristan, Richard, Marny, Bev, Aidan, Carmel, Saghar, Farnush, Jules P, Asherly, Lou, Richard L and so many more… please know I am grateful!

To all the teens and young adults who have so much to say, so much wisdom, care so much for the planet and its humans… and who struggle with the world. Keep meeting, keep talking, keep praying, keep taking action, keep resting, keep serving, keep encouraging, keep including, keep inviting. Holding you all in my heart, whether in this world or the next. LB… you did the right thing! You are amazing! Thank you xxx

Life is full of ups and downs, twists and turns. I hope that when you read this book, and perhaps re-read it, you will find yourself to be of worth, of value... you bring something to this world and you are loved.

If you feel affected by any of the issues or themes raised in this book, do reach out to someone to talk, to connect. Be creative and turn your thoughts into poetry, art, stories... whatever you want to do! Here are some addresses that I think are important. There are others but this is a start. Do call, ask for help and see if there is something in your area that you can be part of that will bring you joy.

Sending love to each and every one of you!
Victoria Jane Leith

samaritans.org
alopecia.org.uk
ageuk.org.uk
young minds.org.uk
headstogether.org.uk
manenough.com
bahai.org
alzheimers.org.uk

Lightning Source UK Ltd.
Milton Keynes UK
UKHW010039230822
407650UK00003B/835